Justin McCarthy

The Rebel Rose

A novel. Part 2

Justin McCarthy

The Rebel Rose
A novel. Part 2

ISBN/EAN: 9783337051365

Printed in Europe, USA, Canada, Australia, Japan

Cover: Foto ©Andreas Hilbeck / pixelio.de

More available books at **www.hansebooks.com**

A Novel.

'Say, pretty Tory, where's the jest
To wear that co our on your breast,
When that same breast confessing shows
The whiteness of the Rebel Rose?'

IN THREE VOLUMES.
VOL. II.

LONDON:
RICHARD BENTLEY AND SON,
Publishers in Ordinary to Her Majesty the Queen.
1888.

CONTENTS OF VOL. II.

THE REBEL ROSE.

CHAPTER I.

STONEHENGE PARK.

THE visit to Lord Stonehenge was arranged to take place about the time of the Whitsun vacation. There was to be a curious collection of guests under the picturesque and ancient roof of the great house of Stonehenge Park. Time was to be given to Sir Victor Champion to be melted by Mary Beaton's charms, and to make an impression on Rolfe Bellarmin. This latter opportunity was to be Champion's *quid pro quo*. ' If you give us a chance of winning you to our money claim, we will give you a chance of winning Bellarmin to your side against the House of Lords.' The position had not been openly defined in bald terms such as these, though that valuable intermediary Tressel had made it his business to throw some subtle hints into the Jacobite conclave. Lord Stonehenge, who had none of the gifts of a politician, and took very little interest in the strife of parties and the manœuvring of leaders in the House of Commons, hardly appreciated the full significance of Tressel's suggestions. He had nothing in common with the Radical Tressel, and had been a good deal surprised to see him turn up at Mary Beaton's reception. Still he was quite aware that, for the sake of Miss Beaton's claims, it would be well to have Tressel's good word in the House, though he did not yet know how or when those claims were to be advanced. He accepted Tressel's ideas, therefore, with polite cordiality; and though no deliberate scheme of the kind would ever have shaped itself in Stonehenge's brain, the true meaning of the visit came to be tacitly recognised by more than one of the party. Mary Beaton and

Rolfe Bellarmin knew least of the immediate political purpose of the visit when the invitation was given. Mary thought it was got up as a pleasant holiday and novelty for her, and, till he came to the house, Bellarmin did not know that Champion was to be his fellow-guest.

Mary Beaton noted with keen and artistic interest all the features of the beautiful region through which they passed. She and her chaperone Lady Struthers, and her cavalier General Falcon, had been brought by special train from London some seventy miles to the nearest station to Stonehenge Park, where they found Lord Stonehenge's carriages, and from which they had still some miles to drive. The country had a sort of cultivated barrenness. There were bluff chalk-hills rising abruptly, and covered with box and gnarled funereal yews ; and below these were green pleasant valleys, and rich apple orchards, and picturesque thatched cottages, and perhaps a quiet stream meandering beneath spreading beech-trees. Now they would come upon a stretch of common with its clumps of black heath, like ill-shapen mounds, and shrubs of gorse lifting golden plumes, and tall bracken spreading its fronds over the dead brown refuse of last autumn ; or now the road would wind round by some wooded hillside where straight green larches and sombre red-stemmed firs lifted their pyramidal tops above the undergrowth of hazel and alder. And oh, how beautiful were the mossy boles of the big trees ! and how delightful it would be to set one's feet on the crisp red-brown carpet of withered leaves, or to lie stretched on the dry moss, and look up to the blue sky through lattice-work of foliage, or watch the gleams of sunlight slanting downwards, and the shadows shifting their pattern, as the wind stirred the boughs overhead ! All these things affected Mary with a curious melancholy interest. It was like passing through some land she had known in childhood, and till now had forgotten, or had seen in some tender dream of the morning. It was all so thoroughly English, but English of the past, and not of the present ; the ideal England which some of us, and she was of the number, would fain believe to have once been real. The girl's eyes were moist ; why, she did not know.

The carriage passed through the lodge-gates, and there was a mile or two of stately pleasaunce, where deer lifted their antlered heads and scampered away among the fine old trees, till at last the house came in sight. Lady Struthers' honest heart swelled with pride and joy at the thought of being welcomed and lodged in such a place. She drew back her shoulders and let her full chest expand, and her eyes sparkled even more brightly than their wont; but she kept her proud and glad emotions to herself. Not for worlds would she have had it supposed that her life from childhood upwards had not been passed in halls with which Stonehenge Park could at best only compete.

'One might be very happy in a place like this,' Mary said, with a sigh. ' It seems so much more real, so much more like a home, than our big dreary barracks of palaces in Germany.'

'Oh, well, of course! there's no place like England,' Lady Struthers affirmed, 'and you as an Englishwoman must feel that as well as I. Lord Stonehenge has quite a nice home of it here ; very nice indeed. It reminds me

a good deal of my aunt's place in Perthshire,'
observed Lady Struthers reflectively. ' She
was my mother's half-sister, and a great
heiress ; and if all had had their dues, her
property should have come to me as the
rightful inheritress. But my uncle married
again, and had a son, at the age of sixty-
five—a woman the family couldn't countenance, my love—and that's how wicked repro-
bates flourish, while virtuous paupers have to
grub along as best they may. I got nothing,'
pursued Lady Struthers mournfully, ' except
a parcel of Mechlin lace and a diamond heart
—the jewel, Madame, which you admire. I
trust my dear mistress and pupil will honour
me and my aunt's memory by accepting it as
a wedding gift, at such time as she shall have
made her choice of a husband, which will, I
am convinced, be in accordance with her
illustrious ancestry. It should have been an
entire *parure*,' and Lady Struthers sighed
deeply, ' if my aunt's wishes had been duly
considered—a *parure* that would have been
worthy to take its place among historic, nay,
even royal jewels ; but bygones must be bygones, as I am always telling General Falcon.

It's not for us poor mortals to keep up ill-feeling when even in Revelations the devil was only let loose for a thousand years.'

General Falcon's eyes spoke scorn of Lady Struthers' maunderings. Just then, however, the carriage drew up at the entrance to Lord Stonehenge's house.

On the steps to receive them stood Lord Stonehenge, and when the carriage stopped, he came down the steps bareheaded, and handed Mary out. With him, a little in the background, were two men—one old and thin and stooped, one young and thin and straight —and a dark-haired, bright-eyed boy. After Lord Stonehenge had handed Mary out and welcomed her, the boy came forward with a smiling face, and the assured grace of one who knows that his turn comes next. Lord Stonehenge presented him to Mary as Don José, Prince of Saragossa.

Don José prettily dropped on one knee, and took Mary's hand and touched it lightly with his lips. General Falcon's heart swelled with exultation. 'We are recognised,' was the thought that passed through his mind. Mary blushed and smiled, was confused and pleased. All this was delightful to Lady Struthers, whose demeanour seemed instantly to acquire an even greater stateliness, and whose curtsey to the young Prince was worthy of the seventeenth century. Lady Struthers disdained the modern bob. 'We might almost fancy ourselves again at the Residenz,' she murmured to her mistress. Then Lord Stonehenge presented Monsignor Valmy and the Rev. Dr. Amblaine, the first of whom, as became a most true and fervent Catholic, Mary greeted with a deep reverence.

Don José was the heir—the recognised heir—of a lost cause. He was the head of the elder branch of an exiled royal family. He was a representative of Legitimacy, of Divine Right. He was like Mary Beaton, in a certain sense, but then he had the advantage over her that his was a country of revolution and hers was not. The Crown might be going a-begging any day in his country; and his house might put in a claim and make it good. He was a claimant of admitted rank and account. Diplomacy kept its eye upon him; he was never quite out of the calculations of European statecraft, of foreign offices and embassies, and chancelleries and drawing-rooms, and coteries and petticoateries. But in Mary Beaton's country no palace revolutions were looked for, and European diplomacy regarded the throne of Queen Victoria as pretty safe. Therefore Mary Beaton, as compared with Don José, was like the niece of a rich man who has any number of healthy children and grandchildren, while Don José was like the nephew of one who has neither chick nor child of his own, but has some few nephews or nieces, all of whom he cordially detests, but some one of whom he will have to choose for the inheritance of his possessions. No doubt any practical politician, in looking shrewdly over the field, would have betted heavily against Don José's chances; but no practical politician would have troubled his head about Mary Beaton at all. Don José was far from being a favourite; indeed, he had the field against him; but Mary was not in the running. That was the difference, and it certainly was a very considerable difference. It particularly impressed itself just now on the mind of Mary

Beaton herself, and she even wondered whether it did not impress itself upon the mind of Lord Stonehenge as well. Mary was not certain yet whether Stonehenge was a mere dreamer and visionary or not.

Stonehenge House was a vast pile of red brick and gray stone; it stood upon the brink of a broad lake. The grounds around were of immense extent; a pine-wood was but an incident in the visitor's drive. Lord Stonehenge, when he was staying at this place, never left his own grounds, never passed beyond his own gates, unless when he had to visit some sick tenant or neighbour—poor neighbour, that is to say, for he did not hold much intercourse with his nearest rich neighbours. One was a newly-made Radical baronet, the other was a no-Popery Tory squire; and Lord Stonehenge naturally did not greatly care for either.

Although Lord Stonehenge was a devoted Catholic, his actual demesne enfolded the parish church and the vicarage, and even the graveyard, where the rude Protestant and Puritan forefathers of the hamlet sleep. He was not unpopular among his Protestant tenantry ; he always acted liberally, and he was not in any sense a bigot. He might have been very popular if he had cared for popularity ; but he loved quietude and ease, and the society of people who thoroughly un-derstood him ; and at present his mind was filled with fancies and dreams—fancies which he tried to discourage, and dreams which used to be day and night thoughts and pro-jects to generations of his ancestors.

The outer door opened into a great hall, almost the full size of the middle block of the house. Ancestral portraits, most of them by famous painters, hung on the walls. Suits or armour and stands of arms were there, the empty mailcoats seeming not inapt represen-tatives, now in their emptiness, of the cause for which they had once been dinted and battered on many a battle-field. The hall had a great stand, in which were grouped sticks and staves and cudgels and stocks of various kinds. Lord Stonehenge had a taste for the accumulation of sticks from all parts of the world. His friends who knew his taste often brought him a present of some desirable and uncommon sort of staff.

It was all new and interesting to Mary. She had never stayed before in a great English house. Her own ancestral home had been sold in her grandfather's time, and it had not occurred to her to regret it; but now, amid her ejaculations of surprise and pleasure, she could not suppress a deep sigh.

'This makes me sad in a kind of way,' she said, turning with her sweet frank smile to Monsignor Valmy, who, standing a little apart, with his thin hands folded before him, and a gentle benevolent curiosity on his somewhat severe countenance, was watching her intently. 'I was so delighted with my little house in Kensington,' Mary went on, 'and so glad because the portraits of some of my own people looked down upon me from the walls, and in England, their own country. But now, after all, when I see this place, I can't help feeling an alien and an exile.'

Lord Stonehenge made a little movement of almost impassioned protest, but he did not speak. Perhaps shyness kept him silent.

'Surely that is an impossibility, Madame, if you turn in this direction,' said Monsignor Valmy, in suave, tender accents, and he motioned towards a part of the hall where hung a collection of Stuart portraits, conspicuous among them a fine likeness of Mary Stuart. This particular painting is said to have been done by a French artist during that brief period when, in the flush of her youth, her loveliness, and her happiness, Mary Stuart presided as Queen Consort at the Court of France. She is represented in the dress of that Court. A royal mantle of crimson velvet, edged with minever, falls from the shoulders; she has the ungraceful puffed sleeves and the more becoming long-waisted jewelled bodice, with high collar and small ruff, which is thrown back, opening deep in front, and shows the shape of her long slender throat. Dark chestnut hair—dark, save for the ruddy tinge running through it—waves upon the broad, candid brow, and is confined by three rows of pearls, with one large pendant drop below the parting. The face, a perfect oval, turns a little towards the left shoulder; the large, dark, almond-shaped eyes have a clear penetrating gaze, and an almost child-like purity. The brows are delicately arched; the nose is fine and straight, and the lips gracious and slightly pouting. In spite of the girlish serenity and sweetness of the countenance, it has that expression of melancholy so characteristic of the royal Stuarts. It was impossible not to be struck by the resemblance Mary Beaton bore to this portrait, even in that very pensive shade which gave so pathetic a charm to her bright young beauty. It was remarked by several. General Falcon looked earnestly from the pictured to the living face. Involuntarily Lady Saxon's words rose in his memory: 'You may be her Bothwell!' A red wave overspread his forehead, through which the scar shone livid.

Monsignor Valmy seemed an appropriate figure against the Stonehenge background. He was Don José's tutor and travelling companion, a Jesuit priest, whose ascetic life was printed in the lines of his thin, clear, wasted face. His hair, which fell almost to his shoulder beneath the biretta which he wore, was prematurely gray. He looked seventy. In reality he was about fifty. He had fine delicately-cut features of the Dantesque type. There was power in his steady serene eyes, and a greater sweetness than subtlety in his smile. He had an air of culture and dignity, and his manner, like that of most Catholic priests of high birth and position, was singularly bland and courteous.

Monsignor Valmy's chaplain and secretary, the Rev. Dr. Amblaine, hung in the background. He was a very young man with a hectic flush, and apparently of a consumptive tendency. Mary heard later from her host that he had, in fact, but poor hope of prolonging his life. He was a scholar, and she heard, too, that he had an almost morbid love of books, and a taste for the personal possession of editions which the public could not easily get at. A little room full of books, all his own—his very own—was his happiness.

The library at Stonehenge, in which they had tea, must, one would fancy, have been a Paradise to poor Dr. Amblaine. It was a great oblong room, with three tall windows looking out on the lake, and its collection of books and manuscripts was almost unique for a private owner's house. But, in fact, it gave little joy to Dr. Amblaine. He had been a few weeks at Stonehenge Park, and was to be there only a few weeks longer. But he had already set up his own little store of books in his own room; and he stole every possible moment to go and look at them, and to take down this one and that from its shelf, and open it tenderly, and pat its cover and stroke its back and study its title-page and its *imprimatur* fondly, and utter little half-articulate and gladsome words over it. Nor did he want to keep his treasures all to himself. He was only too delighted when he could entice some one of the company into his room and win, by gentle extortion, a few words of admiration and of sympathy. All this seemed curiously pathetic to Miss Beaton, when, after she had been some days at Stonehenge, she made him thus happy; and she would not even smile, though Don José did his very best to force her into mirth by his odd interjections and furtive grimaces.

Don José was a clever, sweet, precocious boy of fourteen. He was an odd compound, for he had the frolicsomeness of an English schoolboy, the unleavened conceit and whims of a Parisian lad, and occasionally an interval, short indeed, of the Spaniard's melancholy gravity. When Lord Stonehenge had placed

Mary in a chair near one of the windows, through which floated a gentle breeze from the lake, bearing sweet scent of June roses and honeysuckle on its breath, and was busying himself in getting her tea, Don José rushed forward with a funny little gesture of mock humility.

'No, no!' he exclaimed; 'she is my Princess —the head of my family—the Queen of my house! I am her page. I must pour her wine. I must bring her tea. I and no one else.'

Lord Stonehenge laughed.

'But I am her host, my Prince,' he said.

'No matter,' cried the Prince; and he sprang to the table, poured Mary's tea, and handed it to her, kneeling on one knee the while.

And Mary laughed too, and accepted the homage, and leaned back in her chair, sipping her tea and feeling delightfully at home. She fell into conversation with Monsignor Valmy presently, and asked some questions about the services in the private chapel at Stonehenge. She regretted that she had as yet no chaplain of her own, and that though the Oratory was not far from her house, she attended the offices of her Church less regularly than had been her wont abroad. The priest bent upon her a look of fatherly regard.

'You feel the need of religion?' he said.

'It is difficult to lead the religious life in London,' said Mary thoughtfully.

'And yet it is in London, where material interests and enjoyments throng around us like a vast army of shadowy forms, darkening and vitiating the spiritual atmosphere, that the religious life seems a greater reality as well as a greater need than here, for instance, where the air is pure—morally and physically,' said the priest, with a grave smile.

'Yes, I know what you mean,' cried Mary; 'I feel that it is as you say; we are surrounded by shadows. I often fancy that other people's realities are my shadows. And then to go into the solemn security of our own Church, and to feed our own souls, and give no food to the starving, ignorant souls outside, seems to me no less selfishness than to feed our bodies and let the poor die of hunger at our doors.'

'Madame, you allow your mind to dwell

too much upon the sufferings of the poor,' interposed Falcon abruptly.

'I have often had the thought which Madame's words suggest,' said Lord Stonehenge, in a dreamy tone. 'We rich and exclusive Catholics in England are, in the spiritual sense, like Dives. Well,' he added, in a lighter manner, 'we are introducing one alien presence into our fold here—if not two. When Mr. Bellarmin arrives, he will find himself the only one of the party who is not a Catholic.'

Mary made a little involuntary movement of interest as he spoke. She had been wondering since her arrival in the house whether Bellarmin was already there, and if not, when he was expected. Falcon asked the question, 'When does Mr. Bellarmin come?'

'In a day or two,' replied Stonehenge. 'Presumably, he is less necessary in the House of Commons than Sir Victor Champion, who follows him when the Whitsuntide recess begins.'

'You are right,' Monsignor Valmy said presently, 'in qualifying your remark about the alien presence—in one instance, at least.

Sir Victor is as yet outside the fold, but his instincts are leading him to look over the pale. His mind has in it much of the Churchman; his sympathies are with the Church.'

'I have sometimes thought,' Stonehenge said with a smile, 'that Champion would make an admirable Cardinal.'

'He would like the office, I dare say—many of its functions, at least. But has he not a little too much mysticism, emotionalism, even ecclesiasticism about him to be quite effective as a Prince of the Church?'

'Yet you look to his being Prime Minister of England,' said Stonehenge.

'Oh yes, that is different. In England you govern——'

'*You* govern!' Stonehenge said again with a smile. 'Why don't you say *we* govern? You are an Englishman.'

'Yes; but I am in spirit a mediæval Englishman—an Englishman of the days when England still believed in her saints,' answered Monsignor Valmy.

'Well, you were going to say something when I interrupted you.'

'I was going to say that in England you govern by talking, and therefore Champion is a destined Prime Minister,' said Monsignor Valmy. 'But a Prince of the Church must be trained to the art of silence as well as speech, and do you think Sir Victor could ever learn that? No; he must be always in some place where he can use the great gift which Heaven has given him. He would make a marvellous preacher. If he were one of us,' Monsignor Valmy added meditatively, 'I should like to appoint him to preach in some West-End church, to stir the hearts of the light-minded and to compel Protestants to go and listen.'

'I am afraid there is a very worldly side to Champion's ambition,' Lord Stonehenge said. 'The redemption of souls might serve as an avocation for him; it would never be his vocation.'

'Os homini sublime dedit,' Valmy said quietly. 'A man of genius and heart looks naturally up from the world. Have you seen much of Sir Victor Champion?' he added, turning to Miss Beaton.

'Yes,' she answered; 'he has called on me

several times lately, and we have talked a
good deal together.'

'And you like him; you admire him?'

'Oh yes,' she replied frankly; 'who could
help admiring him? I confess that I like
him best when he puts on that courtier-like
old-world manner which suits him so well.   I
am not so much interested in him when he
talks generalities to me as he might to an
ordinary young London lady, and asks my
plans for the season.'

'Perhaps that is Champion's diplomatic
way of trying to find out something about
you, Madame,' said Lord Stonehenge; 'something about your own and your friends' pro-
jects and ideas, which he might think it
impolitic to ask directly.'

'I would rather he questioned me outright
about what he wanted to know,' said Mary.
'But I think he must have discovered after
the second visit that I did not like him so
well as the man of society, for he became the
courtier again.'

'And Mr. Bellarmin?' pursued the priest
blandly.

'Oh, Mr. Bellarmin'—and Mary's colour

rose slightly—' he too has been to see us three or four times. But Mr. Bellarmin is different. He is younger, naturally more of the London man. Mr. Bellarmin amuses me, and he interests me too ; for he seems to have two sides to his character. I don't feel with him as with Sir Victor, that I ought to be on my best behaviour.' She laughed a half-conscious laugh, which both . Monsignor Valmy and Lord Stonehenge noticed.

Alas for Bellarmin ! It was quite true that, in spite of his prudent resolves, he had found occasion more than once to visit the young Pretendress at her house in Kensington. It would seem uncourteous, unfeeling, he argued to himself, to slight the frank invitations, almost commands, of a lady in Mary Beaton's peculiar position—a stranger in her own country, a victim, so Bellarmin put it, to the accident of her illustrious birth.

At first Miss Beaton was enchanted with everything at Stonehenge Park. She loved to wander over the great old house from room to room, and corridor to corridor. From the foot of the two wide flights of stairs which met in the middle of the hall, one might look up to a glass dome, and through it see the shadow of a little turret that commanded a view of the whole country round. Mary delighted in mounting this tower, and gazing over the broad, fair English landscape on the one side, to the more barren stretch of country, the bleak cliffs and misty sea on the other. She persuaded herself sometimes that she saw on the horizon the outlines of Lady Saxon's eyry, Petrel's Rest. She had thought many times, since that day of her reception, of Lady Saxon, of her brilliancy, her beauty, her vivid intriguing life, and of her frank confession of an occasional longing for solitude and savagery. Somehow Mary thought of Lady Saxon most often in association with Bellarmin, and then the young girl's cheek would flush painfully—she did not dare to ask herself why—and she would shrink and determinedly turn her mind away.

The people at Stonehenge humoured Mary Beaton's fancies, and permitted her to throw completely aside the flimsy pomp and ceremony which, in London, Falcon so strongly insisted upon. Thus, here, she was more of the merry schoolgirl than the dignified young claimant who had declared herself 'every inch a queen.' Lady Struthers remonstrated feebly, but she could not gainsay the Prince of Saragossa and Monsignor Valmy, who took Miss Beaton's view of things. Mary was charmed with little Don José. The boy had picked up some London slang, which he found great pleasure in airing for Mary's amusement and social education. They became comrades, and used to have long rambles and rides together. Still there was want of force, of interest, of movement about all this, and Mary found herself secretly wishing that Mr. Bellarmin would appear. He had not come on the day first appointed, but had put off his arrival two days on the plea of committees and debates.

She wanted him to come before Sir Victor. A day or two of his bright companionship without the constraint of the elder and graver statesman's presence would be pleasant, Mary thought. For Mr. Bellarmin was young, and Sir Victor was—oh, well, not old, not exactly old, but elderly. Sir Victor seemed quite an elderly person to Mary Beaton. She had always been a good deal mixed up with elderly people; she was under the care and in the close companionship now of elderly people, and she yearned for the society of the young, as one weary of gray skies and dun clouds might yearn for the sunshine. Perhaps this condition of feeling, all natural and comprehensible as it was, might serve to account for the fact that elder people sometimes grew a little displeased and impatient with sweet Mary Beaton. They suspected that she yearned for younger companions sometimes, and it made them bitter. Certainly it made General Falcon bitter. General Falcon looked out for the coming of young Bellarmin with alternate sinking of the heart and rising of passion. The mere mention of Bellarmin's name brought a scowl to Falcon's face. He was beginning to fancy that he had been wrong in his first estimate of Bellarmin's position. He had believed him to be enmeshed in Lady Saxon's toils; he now suspected that Lady Saxon's influence was not entirely paramount.

It was evidence of a certain feline craft in Falcon that he should seem to countenance and even encourage any apparent admirer of

Mary Beaton, whereas in reality the serious suggestion of her marriage coming into his mind as a possibility, nay, a certainty in the future, set all his strongest passions at work, and turned him for the time almost into a madman. He had appeared eager to welcome both Bellarmin and Sir Victor Champion to the house in Kensington, and to seize on the evident attraction of both to his charge as a factor in his political schemes ; but now that the attraction seemed to have become more distinct, he regarded it with a mixture of abhorrence and terror. Yet he still placed so severe a restraint upon himself that only Lady Saxon, had she been in his company, could have read the morbid workings of his diseased mind.

CHAPTER II.

AMONG THE LILIES.

FOR days before the Stonehenge visit, Bellarmin's soul had been sorely racked. Soon after he had sent away the fateful letter which was Lady Saxon's trophy, a terrible revulsion of feeling came over him. He felt like one who has sold his soul to the Spirit of Darkness. Never had he been deceived in his cooler moments by Lady Saxon's tenderest protestations and professions. He knew that she did not love him, that she was not a woman to love any one in the true sense. His heart revolted at the thought of her treachery to her husband. He felt himself degraded by the servitude he had allowed her to impose on him, and now from servitude he had made it slavery. He had written to her a declaration of love ; and it was not true ; he did not love her. He was dazzled by her, allured by her, infatuated by her : his senses betrayed him to her ; but he did not love her ; and he knew it now only too well. He had a hideous presentiment that his letter would yet be made to play some part in some scheme of Lady Saxon's. So little faith had he in her, when he was not under the bewildering sway of her presence and her charm, that he actually found this thought taking possession of his mind—the thought that the letter had been drawn from him to be used in some way against him. And added to all this was the feeling that now he had cut himself off from Mary Beaton for ever. Little hope, indeed, had he ever that Mary Beaton could care for him, or that anything could come of it even if she did. But still he was free to think of her, to fill his soul with thought of her, to hold her always in his heart. Now he must try to think of her no more. The bond-slave of Josephine Saxon must not admit the thought

of Mary Beaton into the profaned sanctuary
of his heart.   He felt that such transactions
have their own code of honour, and he must
order his heart so that it should not give out
its feelings to any other woman. 'A man,'
he said to himself savagely, ' ought to be one
thing or the other ; he ought to be either
good or bad ; he ought to have the courage
of his goodness or the courage of his badness ;
he ought to be—not like me '

Bellarmin was for the time distinctly unhappy.   He seemed to have lost interest in
everything.   He was out of tune with political life.   There were moments when he
wished he had never come up to London ;
never got a seat in the House of Commons.
The world, his world, seemed all darkened ;
he could not see the sky or the stars anywhere.   He was as one who suddenly finds
that he has lost sight or hearing or power of
movement, and whose senses are paralyzed
by the appalling knowledge.   He had come
to understand that in the terrible struggle
between the two forces in his nature the
spirit of evil had conquered, but not cast out,
the spirit of good ; that the conquered spirit

lay, a perpetual ache and agony, deep in its prison in his heart.

Still, Bellarmin was young, and whether he would or not, his forces were elastic, and he soon determined to make the best of his Stonehenge visit, to put on an appearance of brightness, to meet Mary bravely, and to be in the world like a man of the world.

These thoughts were in Bellarmin's mind as he came down by the train—the same train which had brought Mary Beaton. He found the party drinking tea in a quaint garden on one side of the house—a garden laid out in fancifully shaped beds, bordered with box, and almost closed in by red brick walls, on which hung big yellow Maréchal Niel and Souvenir de Malmaison roses. The roses were abloom in sunny sheltered regions now; they grew in profusion at Stonehenge, and the very air seemed heavy with them. Lady Struthers was at the tea-table ; General Falcon and Monsignor Valmy were conversing together, and Mary and Lord Stonehenge sat a little apart. They both rose as Bellarmin was ushered towards them, and Lord Stonehenge went forward to greet his guest ; but

Mary held back, looking very stately and slender as she stood beside a bed of tall white lilies, and indeed not unlike the lilies themselves, Bellarmin thought. A little blush came to her cheek, however, when at last Bellarmin shook hands with her.

'I am glad to see you,' she said simply. 'We were beginning to think that you didn't mean to come.'

'Oh,' he answered, 'I have had tiresome committees—a tedious time altogether, with only the consolation of feeling that I was doing my duty—which was not much of a consolation after all, under the conditions—and the satisfaction of knowing that I should get a holiday anyhow at Whitsuntide.'

'Everyone gets holidays at Whitsuntide,' said Mary, 'and then——,' she was going to say, 'and then Sir Victor will be here'—but added, 'we were going to give you a longer holiday.'

'Have you seen Sir Victor Champion?' asked Stonehenge, and felt immediately that the question needed some preparation, for Bellarmin gave a quick, surprised look.

'Seen him ? Yes ; every day. But I have had no particular talk with him.'

'He is coming here in the Whitsuntide recess,' said Lord Stonehenge calmly.

'Coming here !' repeated Bellarmin, still surprised, and glancing at Mary ; 'I did not imagine that I was to meet Sir Victor Champion.'

'You don't object ?' said Lord Stonehenge. 'I know that you differ politically—perhaps not as much as people think. Here, political differences count for as little as those of creed,' and he made a gesture towards the priest. 'You will find Monsignor Valmy a perfectly delightful companion. So I hope you, and Miss Beaton too, will find Sir Victor. I have an idea, Mr. Bellarmin, that if you were in the House of Lords you would sit on the cross-benches in more senses than one.'

Mary laughed, and so did Bellarmin.

'I dare say you are right,' said Rolfe. 'Anyhow, I haven't the faintest dislike to staying in the same house with Sir Victor. Quite the contrary ; it is what I have often wished to do ; but I have never been given the chance.   I am delighted to meet him out-side the field of politics.'

'Mr. Bellarmin!' cried Lady Struthers from the tea-table, handing him at the same time a fragrant steaming cup, and the cream jug, 'it's a fresh brew.   Do you take sugar? though it is not the fashion in England to take sugar, I observe.   The first cup was delicious, Mr. Bellarmin; our second wasn't so good; but this is going to be quite as ex-cellent as the first.   And strawberries?   I always assure foreigners that strawberry squash is really *the* typical English dish!   I tell Madame, Mr. Bellarmin, that there's one good you get by living out of one's own country for a number of years.   You notice things and you get perspective.   If I ever go back to Schwalbenstadt I shall introduce the dear Grand Duchess to English strawberry squash.'

That evening both Mary and Don José were in particularly lively humour.   The girl seemed to have been endued with a spirit of playfulness and innocent gaiety that contrasted with her former vague depression, and which was to Bellarmin peculiarly captivating. The young Prince of Saragossa, still hailing her as his queen, made himself her cupbearer, and poured her wine and waited upon her, somewhat to the embarrassment of Lord Stonehenge's solemn butler. Bellarmin fell into the boy's fancy, and gravely paid homage to the pretty Pretendress. The priests smiled benignantly; General Falcon scowled in sullen dissatisfaction. To Lady Struthers and Stonehenge, each in a different fashion, the proceedings savoured too much of a jest on the sacred subject of divine rights to be altogether agreeable.

But Mary Beaton and Bellarmin were very happy, perhaps neither of them quite knew why. When dinner was over, they all went back together to the drawing-room. The windows stood wide open to the terrace, and the lake shone silvery in the moonlight. Don José vaulted forth, and ran down to the boathouse, where a tiny skiff was moored; and presently they heard his clear boy's tenor ringing out a sort of boat-song in Spanish, which sounded like an invitation to follow him.

Miss Beaton paused a little irresolutely on the sill.

'I am going on the water,' said she, looking back into the room; and then she turned again and sang an answering call.

She had a very sweet but not very powerful mezzo-soprano voice, with a pathetic note in it that struck Bellarmin as peculiarly in harmony with that slightly melancholy strain he had noticed in her character.

'Madame,' said Falcon abruptly, 'you will not trust yourself alone on the lake with the Prince, who, to say the least, is young and heedless.'

'But indeed I shall, my good General,' replied Mary, with pretty wilfulness; 'and we shall sing duets on the water to which you may join chorus from the bank if you please. Lord Stonehenge, let us have coffee in the boat-house; and you gentlemen may talk politics or science or anything you like while Don José and I enjoy ourselves.'

'And I,' said Lady Struthers, 'shall beg to remain indoors if Madame and his Highness will excuse my attendance. The lake has no attractions for me. I am not fond of leading the *vie de canard*, which appears to delight you so in England.'

'We make a virtue of necessity, Lady Struthers,' put in Bellarmin.

' Dr. Amblaine and I will enjoy a game of draughts or a little literary conversation,' went on Lady Struthers. ' The pleasures of intellectual intercourse have not come much in my way since we left the cultivated circle of the Residenz. I must confess that I am disappointed in English society,' and she threw a rebuking glance at Bellarmin. ' It seems to me that the entrée to the highest circles in London, political or social, is far from being a guarantee of *intellectual* distinction.'

' Quite true, Lady Struthers,' answered Bellarmin. ' " You must amuse us," is the first command of smart society. It doesn't say, " You must improve us." '

Miss Beaton went lightly out into the garden, singing still as she walked. Bellarmin followed her. He carried a white knitted cloud.

' Lady Struthers beseeches you to put this on.'

She let him wrap the shawl about her head and shoulders.

'I have never heard you sing before,' he said.

'Oh, I sing very passably, I assure you,' she replied ; 'but I have a perverse and *gamin* taste for street-songs, and General Falcon doesn't encourage me in it.'

'He thinks it unbefitting your——' Bellarmin was going to say 'pretensions' but stopped himself, and added, 'your illustrious descent.'

'Exactly, and there he is wrong. Mary Stuart never thought about what was befitting or unbefitting her dignity; and yet she was always a Queen. That's part of the bore of sham royalty,' Mary added, with a sigh. 'One has, metaphorically speaking, to keep the sceptre and crown perpetually *en évidence*. Now I am sure if your Queen, when she was much younger—say, had taken a fancy to sing "Johnny Peel," or "Up in a balloon, boys," everyone would have thought it quite pretty and nice.'

Bellarmin laughed. Mary turned her bright frank eyes to him. They were sparkling with amusement.

'I have only seen the people in their

wretchedness,' she said, and her face became
suddenly sad again. 'I want to see them in
their places of entertainment. Mr. Bellarmin,'
she clasped her hands with a girlish impulsive
gesture; 'I am going to carry out the most
daring project when I go back to London. I
should shock you so terribly that I long to
tell you what it is. But I dare not. I have
only brought the General to consent by dint of
coaxing and promises of the strictest secrecy.'

'I dare say I can guess,' said Bellarmin.
'A private box at the Oxford or the London
Pavilion.'

'Oh dear no; nothing half so much in the
world. But don't ask me another question.'

Whether by design or accident, they had
made a little detour, and instead of proceeding
straight to the bank of the lake near which
Don José was paddling, they turned up by a
small inlet crossed by an ornamental bridge.

'Tell me,' said Bellarmin, looking at her
in a half-amused, half-earnest manner, 'what
is the meaning of it all?'

'The meaning of it!' Mary repeated; and
she stopped short on the bridge, and looked
up at him. 'The meaning of what?'

'This sham royalty, as you call it. What is it to end in ?'

'*Noblesse oblige*,' said Mary a little haughtily. 'I am the last of the Stuarts.'

'That—! of course. No one doubts it. But——'

He paused. He had a vague impulse to question her that he might discover to what extent she herself was aware of any political or social machinations on the part of her adherents. Though Mary Beaton had been magnet powerful enough to draw him at once to Stonehenge, it puzzled him a little why he had been invited there. He wanted to find out what was expected of him, how far he was supposed to espouse Miss Beaton's claims, why Sir Victor Champion had been asked, whether the meeting between him and Sir Victor had been arranged by the Jacobite clan with a view to furthering the minor Stuart business, or by Champion himself for a greater political purpose. His embarrassed manner quickened Mary's curiosity.

'Well,' she said, 'what is it that you are wondering about ?'

'I'll tell you; I'm wondering about two

things : why General Falcon and Lord Stonehenge were so good as to press me to join this party, and, by the way, why does General Falcon scowl at me so fiercely now that I am here ?' He saw in the moonlight the red blood rise to Mary's face, and overspread its milky whiteness.

'You were asked because—well, I'll be frank with you—because I wanted to have someone new and entertaining and fresh from the outside world about me. I am tired of all these fossilized interests. As for my General, perhaps it is that which makes him cross. I can't be responsible for his whims ; they puzzle me quite as much as they can puzzle you.'

' Madame,' said Bellarmin, with real feeling in his voice, ' I am more than honoured ; I am deeply grateful. If you knew what a sweet and soothing beneficial influence you have over me, you would not be surprised that I thank Heaven for the kindly impulse which made you wish for my company.' There was a little pause. It seemed to Bellarmin that the red deepened on Mary's half-averted cheek.

'And the other thing you were wondering about?' she asked presently.

'The other thing! Oh! why is Sir Victor Champion coming?'

Mary looked round at him with a bright little laugh.

'Well, I don't mind confiding to you the least little faint hint of a very tiny political conspiracy, which Lord Stonehenge got from Mr. Tressel, and which he let out to me only yesterday. Mr. Tressel just suggested that Sir Victor would not be sorry to see something of you in a friendly, informal way. Oh, Mr. Bellarmin, it is too delicious that *I* should be mixed up in your English Parliamentary intrigues! I wish you were on Sir Victor's side. I believe in him.'

'You wish I were on his side?' said Bellarmin slowly.

'Not against your convictions, of course; I think, on the whole, that what interests me about you is that you are a *franc-tireur*. Still, I believe I should not be sorry if your convictions were to take the same form as Sir Victor's.'

'You believe that he has sincere convictions ; that he has the good of his country at heart ?'

'Oh, I am certain of it ! No one could watch his face and see the light kindle in his eyes when he talks of what is near his heart, and not feel that he is intensely in earnest. I have seen him several times lately. He is very good in explaining things to me, and he has such a pretty way of recognising me as a Stuart, and all that, as if he were indulging the whim of a child he was fond of. Oh yes, I believe in Sir Victor. I am a little afraid of him. I shall not dare to be frivolous before him as I am this evening; but I admire him immensely, all the same.'

The thought came into Bellarmin's mind, as he walked along by Mary Beaton's side, that it was curious these two women, Josephine Saxon and Mary Beaton—women as unlike in character and temperament as if they had been born in different planets, and showing that dissimilarity most, it seemed to him, in the strange conflicting influence they exercised upon himself—should both feel such genuine and apparently intuitive confidence in Champion's political sincerity. Josephine's frank admission of a former acquaintance with Champion dispelled any dark suggestions that might have rankled in Bellarmin's mind. Her arguments and her appeal in their late interview had, almost unconsciously to himself, affected him strongly. Now they seemed to receive additional strength from the fact of Mary's partisanship. It was a curious convergence of opposing forces. Mary's enthusiastic expressions grated slightly upon him, but they set him thinking. If this bright, intelligent girl were so imbued with belief in Champion's high purpose, was he right in refusing to hear what Champion had to bring forward in his own support? They had crossed the bridge, and now, by a turn in the shrubbery they had been skirting, came suddenly upon the boat-house—a kind of open pavilion with tables and lounges, where the gentlemen were sitting and enjoying their cigarettes, and where coffee was being served. Mary did not wait for any coffee, but stepped into the canoe in which Don José was established, and presently the two had paddled out into the lake.

Monsignor Valmy and Lord Stonehenge

called out admonitions to keep near the shore.
The boy and girl laughed and murmured
together, and in a few moments their voices
burst on the still, soft night, blending in a
rollicking Rhine song.   It was very charming
and poetic, Bellarmin thought.   He sat somewhat apart, near the wide entrance arch of
the pavilion, silent and dreamy as he smoked
his cigar, and gazed at the white figure in the
boat, and the noble head and the play of
features and eyes which seemed spiritualised
by the moonlight.   The two young people
went on, singing song after song, pushing out
into the lake, so that their voices sounded
softer and more distant ; and now they turned
a little point and were hidden by a drooping
willow, though the sweet, ringing melody told
that they were not far.   After a while they
stopped singing altogether.   It could be seen
that they had landed on an islet in the middle
of the lake, where there were more willows
and another pavilion.

Meanwhile the men had fallen into general,
half-political talk, and the question of Mary
Stuart Beaton's inheritance was brought up.
General Falcon was explaining the position

to Monsignor Valmy, and while the echo of Mary Beaton's and Don José's first duet still lingered in his ear, Bellarmin was roused from his dream-like reverie by a pointed question.

CHAPTER III.

' TELL me, General Falcon,' Monsignor Valmy said quietly, ' what you want Sir Victor Champion to do—what you want Mr. Bellarmin to do.' He looked towards Bellarmin as he spoke in a manner that plainly invited Bellarmin to take part in the discussion.

'Am I in this?' Bellarmin asked, half rising, and then drawing his chair nearer to the little group, which was gathered round a small table, on which coffee and cigarettes were placed.

'Surely; I was just saying to General Falcon that we should all like to know what he wants you, for example, to do in regard to these claims.'

'You see, we assume your sympathy and willingness to help us,' Lord Stonehenge said.

'I shall be only too glad to help you,' Bellarmin replied, 'if I can see my way.'

'Exactly; we want General Falcon to give you the light to help you to see your way.'

'Dry light, as Bacon puts it,' Monsignor Valmy said quietly; 'light free from all colouring matter, I suppose Bacon meant. We want to give you that sort of light and none other. We want to have the case put fairly before you, so that you shall judge for yourself on the facts.'

'I have studied the question pretty closely,' Bellarmin answered, 'and very sympathetically. It seems clear to me that there is no constitutional or legal claim, in the technical sense of the words.'

'Mr. Bellarmin doesn't understand the question,' Falcon interposed, with harsh voice and scowling face.

'I have studied it to the best of my ability, General Falcon,' Bellarmin said, determined not to lose his temper. 'If I don't understand it, that is the fault of my intellect and not of my effort. It is well to have everyone's opinion.'

'Oh yes; go on, please, Mr. Bellarmin!' Stonehenge exclaimed, turning eyes of expostulation on the impatient Falcon.

'I am particularly anxious to hear Mr. Bellarmin's full and candid expression of opinion,' Monsignor Valmy said gravely. 'He is one of our friends, General Falcon, not one of our enemies.'

'I ask Mr. Bellarmin's pardon,' said Falcon, in a strange contradictory flash of penitence which puzzled Bellarmin. 'I know he means to be a friend.'

'Now, Mr. Bellarmin,' Lord Stonehenge interposed, a little impatiently.

'I don't see any claim that you could possibly sustain in any court of law, for instance,' Bellarmin explained. 'I don't see how the Government——'

'The Crown?' Monsignor Valmy suggested.

'Oh, well—it isn't the Crown really—it is the Government. The Crown will, as a

matter of public policy, decline to do anything but what the Government advises.
Now it seems to me that as a question of
generosity there is a strong case—and as a
question of public policy, even, a very good
case.   I think in this instance generosity and
public policy would go together.'

'Generosity!' Lord Stonehenge began, in
a doubting tone of voice.

'Yes, I was coming to that point,' Bellarmin went on.   'Are you disposed to make
an appeal to the generosity of the country?
Would you be willing to do that?   Would
Miss Beaton consent?'

'Do you mean, to make an appeal *in formâ
pauperis?*   Is that what Mr. Bellarmin re-
commends?' cried Falcon.

'No, General Falcon.   I didn't recom-
mend anything of the kind.   I didn't re-
commend anything, in point of fact.   I only
asked a question or two, for the guidance of
myself and of all of us.   It is one thing to
make a legal claim in a court of law or even
in Parliament.   It is another to appeal to
Parliament for fair play and moral justice and
generosity—in a matter where it is frankly

admitted that we have no legal claim—I mean legal in the narrow and technical sense.'

'I think Mr. Bellarmin is putting the case very well,' said Monsignor Valmy.

'I am afraid he is putting it only too well—too accurately, I mean,' Lord Stonehenge added.

'Well, my idea is this,' Bellarmin went on, 'I think the claim could be put in that way, in such a manner as to command the attention and sympathy of the House of Commons ; and I don't say that a resolution might not be carried recommending the case to the consideration of the Government ; then, of course, all would depend on the action of the Government.'

'In other words,' Monsignor Valmy said, 'it would depend on who were the Government.'

'Precisely.'

There was a pause full of meaning. The same thought was in the minds of each of the men.

'Yes,' said Lord Stonehenge, with a sudden vivacity of emphasis ; 'it would all depend on who were the men in the Government—I

23—2

mean on who was the man at the head of the Government.'

Bellarmin understood clearly. He thought it would be well to let his listeners know that he understood.

'Now,' he said slowly, 'we are on the eve of a crisis of some sort. Everyone is agreed upon that, and what everyone says does now and then happen to be true—at least, it is unsafe to count on its never coming true. I don't think it would be well to bring up this claim under unfavourable circumstances. Better wait a little, perhaps. Our modern Tories have utterly forsworn or forgotten all memory of their ancient traditions, and the King over the Water. The more stolidly Tory they are, the more inveterately they are opposed to any recognition of a—well—a past condition of things. It would not be of much use trying on anything under them. But suppose there should be a change of Government ?'

'Yes,' Monsignor Valmy observed quietly, 'suppose there should be.'

'There may be before long,' Lord Stone-henge said significantly.

'In other words,' Bellarmin said, taking a long puff at his cigarette, and sending the smoke out before him straight as the path of a bullet; 'suppose Sir Victor Champion were to come into office?'

'As Prime Minister?' Monsignor Valmy inquired blandly.

'As Prime Minister—yes. I suppose he will either come in as Prime Minister or not come in at all.'

'In that case, Lord Stonehenge,' Monsignor Valmy asked with a tone of ingenuous curiosity, 'how do you think Sir Victor Champion would be affected towards these claims?'

'In that case,' Stonehenge answered gravely, 'I should hope favourably—after a while, at least.'

'Yes,' said Bellarmin meditatively. The answer he had received was exactly what he had expected. Their hopes were centred on Champion.

'Will Champion carry the country with him?' Monsignor Valmy asked, still in a tone of simple artlessness.

'In what?' Bellarmin rejoined with manner equally guileless.

Monsignor Valmy smiled.

'For myself,' Lord Stonehenge said abruptly, with the air of one who comes daringly to what others are only thinking of, 'I would much rather see the House of Lords reformed than reorganized—and reformed or reorganized by its friends than by its enemies. Champion has a highly cultivated mind, and he has a deep vein of sympathy in his nature. I prefer Champion as a reformer to—to Mr. Tressel, for instance.'

The priest gave a little shudder.

'The plain common sense of the thing then,' said Bellarmin, 'is that we should keep these claims quiet until we see whether Sir Victor Champion is likely to come into power soon ?'

'May I ask who are understood by "we"?' General Falcon demanded angrily.

'We ? Well, I meant those who are anxious to see justice done to Miss Beaton's claims,' Bellarmin answered with perfect good humour.

'I was delighted to hear Mr. Bellarmin include himself in the number,' put in Monsignor Valmy.

'So was I,' added Lord Stonehenge, with a courteous bend of the head to Bellarmin.

'Only I did not quite understand,' said Falcon, not altogether appeased. There was a pause. Lord Stonehenge broke it.

'We were thinking of something of that kind—of waiting quietly until we see what Champion will do and what will happen. But we are not what are called practical politicians, Monsignor Valmy and I—and I am sure General Falcon would be very angry with me if I were to call him a practical politician.'

'I am a soldier,' said General Falcon.

'Exactly,' Monsignor Valmy rejoined sweetly. 'And I am a priest. We are neither of us qualified to advise Lord Stonehenge on a question of practical politics, and so we are all grateful for Mr. Bellarmin's advice.'

Apparently the matter was regarded as settled. The claims were bound up for the present with the fortunes of Sir Victor Champion's next move, whatever that might turn out to be.

Bellarmin removed his cigarette from his

mouth, and thoughtfully laid down the smouldering end. He looked round the little group.

'I should like to ask one thing—I ask it in all sincerity and faith, and with the fullest friendliness. These claims—these particular claims—are an end, and not a means?'

The priest, who had been gazing abstractedly out on the lake, the clear-cut outline of his ascetic features defined against the dim leafy background, turned to Bellarmin with a ray of keen interest lighting his face into a look of less other-worldliness.

'Do we quite understand?' he asked softly.

'*I* don't understand,' Falcon exclaimed bluntly.

Lord Stonehenge turned to Bellarmin.

'Do you mean, Mr. Bellarmin, that these claims are all that we consider ourselves, on Miss Beaton's part, entitled to make—that on their being satisfied we are prepared to give a receipt in full? If that is what you mean—yes; certainly.' Nevertheless, Lord Stonehenge sighed as he spoke; and the spirit of his ancestors, loyal to the death to

Stuarts of old time, seemed to glow in his refined Vandyke face. ' These money claims are final,' he went on in a tone of determined resignation. 'We have no other money claims to make. The Princess—Miss Beaton —only wants what is her own by right.'

' Yes ; all that I quite understand. But what I would ask is, whether there is any idea of making these claims a sort of test of public feeling as to other possible claims—I am sure you understand my meaning. Believe me, such an idea would end in nothing but utter disaster, ridicule and disgrace.'

' Disgrace !' Falcon cried, his eyes aflame with wrath.

' Yes, General Falcon,' Bellarmin replied, turning to him with some warmth ; ' disgrace to the advisers who ruined a just claim, and exposed to public odium the noblest of— clients '—he was going to say ' women,' but somehow he preferred to leave the sex out of the question—'the noblest of clients, by mixing both up with absurd and hopeless dynastic intrigues.'

Monsignor Valmy's pale, delicate complexion seemed to deepen a little in th moonlight as Bellarmin spoke these words. Lord Stonehenge remained quite self-possessed.

' Mr. Bellarmin,' he said, ' is naturally afraid of being mixed up with a Stuart restoration scheme in the nineteenth century.'

' No, indeed,' Bellarmin broke in warmly. ' I was not thinking of myself—I could go into a scheme or keep out of it, just as I thought best to do. I was not thinking of danger—of real danger—for—for anybody. I was thinking of ridicule. I was thinking of public odium—so hard for a woman to bear.'

The sex which he would fain have kept out of the controversy here boldly asserted itself, and came in.

' I was thinking of all that—and of the inevitable ruin of these very claims themselves, no matter how just they may be. That is what I was thinking of, Lord Stonehenge.'

Again there was a pause ; and through the silence of the arbour there floated the sound of Mary Beaton's laugh as she chatted with the young Prince—that sweet frank laugh which, with all its sweetness and its girlishness, had in it an imperious ring. Involuntarily, at its sound, the men moved forward a little — all except the priest, and he remained still, with that bland inquiring smile on his thin lips, as if there were in his mind no thought of the girl round whom centred these curious out-of-date suggestions of conspiracy and revolution. They could see the boat as it lay like a fairy skiff on the shining lake, and the slim youth with his picturesque Spanish face, and the slender, proud, bright maiden, whose dark wavy hair and contour of feature and smile and gesture seemed to have in them something traditional, which woke in the mind memories of Holyrood and of reckless, winsome Mary Stuart. How out of keeping with the commonplace fret, the vulgar rush and scurry of nineteenth-century existences, were these two living representatives of dead dynasties! It had an odd, bewildering effect —this spell of the past. Bellarmin felt a tightening of his heart, he scarce knew why; and then a rush of impetuous desire to bear her away from it all—from the network of scheming and calculations and false hopes and associations that were at once tragic and poetic and absurd. He longed to sweep away the glamour of her Stuart ancestry, the poor pretence of princess-ship, and to appeal to her bravely, honestly, as the tender, true-hearted simple English girl that she was—that, and nothing else. For it had come to this with Bellarmin in certain moods of reaction, when the other wilder passion lost its sway over him. These thoughts were moving him to the very depths of his being while Lord Stonehenge said gently :

'I quite understand, Mr. Bellarmin. I didn't put my meaning well—at least, I certainly did not mean to say that you were concerned about yourself. What I meant was that you were afraid some unwise political schemes—or dynastic schemes, if you like— might be astir. But you may be quite reassured. Monsignor Valmy and I—and General Falcon, of course—are sane men.'

'Leave me out!' Falcon exclaimed impatiently. 'I would go my own way if I could.'

Bellarmin made a movement as if he would pull himself out of dreamland, a gesture not lost upon Falcon.

'You see,' Bellarmin said. 'There was some ground for my misgivings, after all.'

'None whatever,' General Falcon retorted. 'I would go my own way if I could—but I can't; and I understand that as well as any practical politician who ever lived. Only I don't want to be taken as approving of every arrangement which I accept just because I can't have any other.'

Monsignor Valmy interposed:

'It is not easy, perhaps, for Mr. Bellarmin to realize our position. We have nothing to renounce—I mean, there is nothing which it is in our power to renounce. No declaration on her part could make the Princess— could make Miss Beaton other than what she is. Suppose she were to say that she renounced being a woman—would she not be a woman all the same? Suppose you were to say you renounced your right to be your father's son, would you be any less the son of your father?'

'All that I can quite understand, looking at it from your point of view—of course mine is quite different.'

'With you it is only like the case of a man

who withdraws from the candidature for the
Presidentship of the United States, or the
office of Lord Mayor of London,' Lord
Stonehenge suggested, with a quiet smile.

'Well, yes, if you like to put it in that way
—yes, I believe in the right of a people to
choose its own chief magistrate, whether
for perpetuity or for four years or one
year.'

'And you a Tory!'

'A Tory Democrat,' Monsignor Valmy
suavely interposed.

'A Tory who believes that the world goes
round, and that something must come of the
discovery of the electric light,' Bellarmin said.
'But what I was going to say was, that I quite
understand your principle, and that I greatly
respect it. All that I want to impress on you
is this—I am only talking now of Parliamentary affairs; it would be absurd of me to
offer you advice in any other matters—I only
want to impress upon you that your last chance
for your real claims—excuse me, I mean your
money claims—would be gone with the House
of Commons—gone with Sir Victor Champion
—gone with any and every English statesman

if the claims were accompanied with the faintest—the very faintest—whisper of dynastic intrigues or even hopes.'

'There are no intrigues,' Lord Stonehenge said slowly and distinctly ; 'none whatever. I think I may tell you also, Mr. Bellarmin, that to men like Monsignor Valmy and myself there are no hopes within the range of any horizon that the eyes of our intellect can compass. If the right order of things is ever to be restored, it will not be in our time.'

'It will be in Heaven's time,' Monsignor Valmy said, bending his head.

'We of this day and generation can do nothing.'

'That is quite enough,' Bellarmin replied gravely. 'You have satisfied all my scruples and fears. Pray forgive my bluntness ; I had to ask these questions.'

Even while they were speaking, General Falcon had abruptly quitted the pavilion. It was evident that even if he had no hopes, he was not willing to admit the fact. Bellarmin was the first to observe that he had gone. Bellarmin said nothing then on the subject ;

but in his mind the ways of Falcon boded trouble.

To Mary Beaton also Falcon's manner seemed ominous. In truth, she had been puzzled and vexed by his fitful moods of late, his strange alternations of capricious fault-finding and jealous affection. It was a relief sometimes to turn to Lord Stonehenge, in whom she always found a grave, respectful devotion and care for her interests, which in many ways appeared more abstract than personal. She had come to rely upon him in an undemonstrative fashion almost more than upon any other of her counsellors, and the thought had flashed through her mind several times during the past week or two that if she were in any real difficulty, it would be to Lord Stonehenge that she would apply for advice.

He was waiting for her alone at the little landing-place when the skiff shot to shore, and the young Prince of Saragossa, with his exaggerated air of deference, bent on one knee to the ground, and held the boat steady while Mary Beaton stepped on land.

' Madame,' said Stonehenge, ' I think that you have been long enough out of doors.

There is a mist rising, and we must be careful of your health.'

'It is you!' exclaimed Mary. 'I thought that solitary figure could only be Falcon, waiting to rebuke me for my misdeeds. Has he commissioned you to scold me? Now I am sure that you have all been talking politics and discussing my claims, and the rest. And Mr. Bellarmin took the sober nineteenth-century, House-of-Commons view of the matter; and my poor General was indignant, and went off in wrath! Wasn't it so?'

'We were discussing your claims, Madame.'

'And you all quarrelled over them?'

'No; we did not quarrel. We came to the conclusion that it was best to let them rest, as far as Parliament is concerned, till a Prime Minister came in who would give them his sympathy and support, and that may be before long.'

'And the Prime Minister will be Sir Victor Champion! I think I can count upon his sympathy, if I can count on nothing else. Well, it was a wise conclusion to come to,

Lord Stonehenge; but I am afraid it did not suit General Falcon's temper, which seems irritated against us all—myself included. Then he went away in anger, and he left you as his deputy to give me my scolding. I am quite accustomed to being found fault with, and made angry, so that you need not have any scruples about beginning.'

'Madame, I could not be so presumptuous, unless anything serious—if it were a question of your safety; and then——'

'And then?' repeated Mary, looking up at him as she moved on by his side.

'And then, Madame,' he said, in a tone very unusual in him, 'I think it would be easier to die for you than to make you angry.'

She felt the thrill of his emotion; it alarmed and bewildered her a little. Was he, too, becoming melodramatic? She glanced up at him again in a troubled way, and her voice changed as she answered, with an attempt to speak lightly:

'One at least of your name, Lord Stonehenge, vowed his life to the service of a Stuart, and he gave it up at Newbury. I was looking at his portrait yesterday, and do you know that your face and his are very much alike ? But those days are past,' she added, ' happily for you and for me.'

' Their ;spirit lives yet,' said Stonehenge, ' and it will endure in me so long as my life endures.'

He stopped and gazed at her solemnly, she, too, standing still. A shaft of moonlight pierced the thick foliage of a little grove through which they were passing to the house, and fell upon Mary's fair face and noble form. The white scarf had dropped from her head, but she held it loosely with her two hands interlaced at her breast. Stonehenge bent forward, and, taking one of her hands in his, stooped low over it, and touched it with his lips.

' Madame,' he said, with an old-world chivalry which might have befitted the cavalier who had fallen at Newbury, ' this is my act of homage to the queen and to the woman. In all faith and sincerity, I lay my heart and my life at your feet. They are yours to do with what you will.'

The young girl started and crimsoned

deeply, and the tears gathered in her eyes. She hardly realized the meaning of his words; she only felt that he was intensely in earnest. She did not know whether this was a part of the fantastic dream—the romantic fealty of subject to sovereign, which even in these prosaic times seemed the birthright of Stuart blood—the rich breath of perfume from the still unfading white rose; or was it the red rose of love which was held out to her—the mere every-day offer of marriage from man to woman? She could have wept aloud in the feeling of strangeness and loneliness and odd humiliation that came over her. What was she, that this man should rate her so high? Would he feel the same to her if she were only Mary—Mary, with no noble name, no historic lineage? Was she any better off, after all, in her sham royalty than the princesses who could never know what it was to be loved for themselves alone?

'Lord Stonehenge,' she cried impulsively, 'why do you think of me like that? I'm not a queen; and I can't accept your life, or—or anything except your friendship, and that I do value with my whole heart. It is more

to me than even you perhaps could understand.'

'I feel glad and happy to hear you say
that,' he answered quietly. 'Since friendship
is the name you prefer, we will call it so;
but, Madame, I want you to know fully that
everything else is included. What *I* call it
does not matter to you, and need never cause
you a moment's responsibility or uneasiness,
since in future it will not be for me to ask,
but for you to demand, or to bestow if
you think good. That is the privilege of
queens, you know,' he added, with a gentle
laugh.

They walked on for a few moments in
silence, and then, as if determined that she
should feel no doubt or embarrassment, he
resumed his ordinary manner, and began to
tell her the subject of their conversation in
the pavilion.

'I don't understand General Falcon,' said
Mary thoughtfully; 'his manner is so strange
and variable. In truth,' she went on, 'I do
not know what he wants of me—or for me.
I sometimes fancy, Lord Stonehenge, that he
is so anxious to have these money claims

settled because, living in London, we are spending more than we ought, and getting to the end of our resources.'

'Oh no, Madame,' interposed Stonehenge hastily. 'Surely you need not be troubled about that !'

'It does not trouble me, even if it were the case. I don't suppose that I shall come to the workhouse, anyhow. And what right have I to be better off than thousands of poor creatures ? What does make me unhappy sometimes is that I seem to have so little to give away. I see so much misery, and I can do nothing to remedy it.'

Mary sighed deeply. They entered the house just then ; Lady Struthers, heroically waiting her young mistress's pleasure, was nodding in the inner hall in company of the Reverend Dr. Amblaine, whom the bonds of courtesy still detained.

The poor priest found no sympathetic soul in Lady Struthers, but he had talked to her about his beloved books all the same, and had accepted the receipt for a cough mixture which had benefited an hereditary prince. And then he had watched her as she nodded, and had pondered upon the emptiness of an existence such as hers. Mary Beaton, graver than was her wont, bade them good-night, and went at once to her own apartments.

CHAPTER IV.

'WHAT WOULD YOU HAVE ME DO?'

MARY BEATON came down to breakfast the next morning apparently in as light spirits as at dinner the previous evening. She chattered frivolously to Bellarmin, and playfully abused him for acting the Tory and being at heart the Radical. She, too, had determined that her manner should give no indication of any serious thought about him, either personal or political, and if occasionally they both relapsed from their prescribed parts, it was only when they were alone, and, so to speak, off their guard. She teased the Prince of Saragossa, and rallied Falcon upon his unsociability in a way that certainly did not tend to put that veteran into good humour. To the two priests and Lord Stonehenge she was quite different—womanly, sweet, and faintly deferential. It was as if she wished the priests to understand that she reverenced their office, and to convey to Lord Stonehenge that his curious outburst of the night before had made no impression upon her, except to increase her friendly regard.

This was not quite the case, however. Mary had passed a perturbed night, and was putting some strain upon herself this morning. Of course she knew now that it rested with her to become Lord Stonehenge's wife. She had no thought of being his wife. She had never considered such a prospect as within the range of things possible to her. But she was touched, nevertheless—the more touched because he had wooed her so delicately, and in such courtier-like fashion. She knew that he would never definitely press his suit ; and he had so phrased it as to leave her the choice of accepting his true meaning. He had given her to understand that it was for her if she pleased to stretch out her hand to him, as might a queen whose rank did not permit her lover to approach her on equal terms ; and he had also made it clear to her that if she did not choose to regard him in the light of a lover, she had the right to demand, and it would be his joy to tender, the loyalty and devotion of a subject.　Such chivalrous homage, far-fetched though it might be, was well calculated to thrill the heart of a young girl with womanly pride and tender exultation.

A little later, Falcon, with much formality, requested an audience.　Mary bade him come to her in the boudoir of the suite of apartments which Stonehenge, with much forethought and study of her fancies, had caused to be arranged for her use.　She was tired, and a little overwrought and preoccupied, and in no mood for his querulous reproaches on her thoughtless way of talking, her want of dignity, her failure to appreciate the gravity of the occasion, and the necessity for ruling her conduct in such a manner as to further the objects they had in view, instead of retarding them.

'You have not come to Stonehenge Park for a mere holiday, Madame,' said Falcon, in a tone severe as though he were chiding a naughty schoolgirl. 'It is not only for amuse-ment that the guests under this roof have been brought together.'

'Indeed, General, there seems to me little likelihood of amusement under this roof or any other, while you represent the skeleton at the feast. I thought that when people went out of town for the Whitsuntide recess they usually called it a holiday.'

'You understand my meaning perfectly, Madame. You were not so blind to your interests when we first came to London.'

'To judge by your manner, General Falcon,' retorted Mary, 'I did not seem to play my part any more to your satisfaction in London than I appear to do here.'

'Oh, I wish you would play a part—any part that pleases you, so long as you chose it out and kept to it, Madame,' replied Falcon gruffly. 'But you act a dozen different parts a day, just as the humour takes you.'

'Assign me a part then, my good Falcon, and I'll do my very best to play it and to keep to it for the whole of this day.'

'I want you to impress that young man Bellarmin more than you do. He is a rising man, they tell me, and he might do service. He seems well inclined.' Mary glanced at Falcon in surprise ; there seemed to her something covert, dangerous in his tone—a sort of studied self-repression. He corrected himself. '*I* don't like him,' exclaimed the old man, with a sudden gesture that betrayed more than the words. ' I suffer when I see him with you, my Princess,' he went on with something of pathetic appeal. ' It wounds me ; it offends me ; it is sometimes more than I can bear.'

' You—General ?' began Mary falteringly. ' How—what would you have me do ?'

' My liking or my disliking is not to the point,' Falcon answered, resuming his former tone. ' Everything, everything of that sort should be subservient to your interest. We are playing a game—a great political game.'

' So you have often told me,' said Mary wearily ; 'and in good truth, General, I am tired of the pastime.'

' That is how you regard it ! Yes ! Crowns, hearts, fortunes, the divine rights which you have inherited from your ancestors—what are they to you? Only a part of the pastime, which you relished at first, and which is now becoming tiresome to you!' He paused for a moment. Mary stood silent—conscience-stricken perhaps. 'Madame, I want you to impress this young man, whose political influence can be turned to our service. You have your part to play towards him, as towards Champion, Tressel—the rest. Is it too much to ask that you will play it becomingly?'

A demure little smile flickered on Mary's lips. She said, with a spark of girlish mischief, 'I had a faint hope, General, that I was making some sort of impression on Mr. Bellarmin.'

'Is that your sense of what is befitting for you?—you! that you should act the schoolgirl—the hoyden; run about the garden at night, play silly pranks; sing music-hall songs——'

Mary flushed a deep crimson. She drew herself up in as stately a fashion as he could have wished. 'Now, General Falcon, you go too far. We have had enough of this.'

'Madame, if I go too far, as you say, it is because, for the sake of your dignity, I dare to make you angry. I speak, at least, with the authority which was committed to me by your father.'

Any allusion to her dead parents instantly turned the current of Mary Beaton's displeasure. 'Well?' she said in a softer tone. 'But speak gently; and remember'—she hesitated and smiled again, this time sadly—'remember that I am only a girl.'

'Madame,' he replied, not noticing her last words, 'you know what I mean. The pretty levity which might very fittingly attract a man of Sir Victor Champion's age and great qualities and renown, and to which in that case I have nothing to say, would be out of place with a man so much younger, so much less distinguished. I want you to impress Mr. Bellarmin with the sense of your position; of your personal dignity as well as the dignity which you inherit. I want you to show yourself a princess—the descendant of a line of kings. He comes of the middle-class—that hateful English middle-class! They respect only those who look down on them and keep them at a distance. A man must be a gentleman—more, an aristocrat, to understand that a princess may be friendly with him, and remain a princess still.'

'Mr. Bellarmin seems to me a very perfect gentleman,' said Mary. 'Quite a chivalrous sort of youth, and on the old feudal pattern. Is that English middle-class? Well, I approve of English middle-class. And Sir Victor Champion—he is not middle-class then, since I am to be permitted a touch of levity in my manner to him?'

'You wilfully misunderstand and mock at me. Levity is too strong a word. I should not have used it. You have a certain manner —ah, I know its charm!—a girlish impulsiveness, which, to a statesman of mature years, would be but a delicate compliment, a condescension——'

'I see. Rank may stoop to elderly renown. But tell me—I am curious—is Sir Victor Champion middle-class?'

'He comes of the middle-class. Yes.'

'Then through all my condescension, I must impress him too with a sense of my dignity?'

'You must, Madame. I especially request it.'

'Observe, I want to learn my part, which seems a complicated and rather contradictory one. Is there anybody else, General Falcon, to whom I may be affable, or must be haughty—anyone who is to be impressed with a sense of my dignity?'

'Yes, there is, Madame—one for whom it is far more needed than for any other.'

'Indeed, dear Falcon; and who may that person be?'

'Yourself, Madame.'

Mary laughed gleefully.

'I thought we were coming to that,' she said. 'Well, now, what about Lord Stonehenge?' Her voice faltered a little; she gave him a furtive glance from beneath her drooped lashes. 'How am I to comport myself with regard to him? He is an aristocrat—I suppose you will concede that—and equal to drawing subtle distinctions. Is it to be a case of dignity or impudence?'

'Madame!'

'Don't be shocked. I was only alluding to the name of a picture—Landseer's—don't you remember?'

'No, Madame, I don't,' said Falcon decisively, with the air of one who turns the picture to the wall. 'But I wanted to speak to you about Lord Stonehenge. I am glad you brought up his name.'

'I am glad I did anything right, General. Well?'

'Play off Champion, and—yes—and this young Bellarmin, against Stonehenge and the priests,' Falcon said, with a sudden vehemence that almost startled Mary, accustomed as she was to his changing moods. 'Let Stonehenge see that you have other friends.'

'I don't understand you at all this time, my good Falcon. Tell me what you do mean?'

'I don't distrust Lord Stonehenge,' Falcon said hurriedly; 'I don't wish you to distrust him; but we must show him that we have other friends. About these money claims he is of no use at all. He can't be of any use. We must look to Champion for that. Lord Stonehenge had better get to know that, and be reminded that there are higher claims that not he, nor any man on earth, must talk of compromising.'

'General Falcon,' Mary spoke very gravely,

'I cannot understand why you speak in such a way of Lord Stonehenge. If any woman ever had a true friend, I have one in Lord Stonehenge. Do you think I don't know that? He is as true to me as—as yourself.' She turned on him a searching, half-alarmed look, which seemed to disconcert Falcon, for he lowered his eyes to the ground. 'I will play no part with him—or—with anybody. I will be myself; what God made me. Princess or no Princess, what do I care? Ah, yes, I do care! Do not be afraid, General, that I shall act in any way unworthy of my Stuart blood. I will keep my own self-respect. I will not stoop to intrigue or double-dealing. I am a Stuart, yes—but I am an honest English girl, and—and—I will not play off Mr. Bellarmin against Lord Stonehenge, or Lord Stonehenge against Mr. Bellarmin ; or Sir Victor against either—oh, you make things too hard for me! Is there nothing due to myself? Am I to have no consideration? Because I am a Stuart, and have claims—and rights—which sometimes—Heaven forgive me!—seem as shadowy and unreal as if I were a stage-princess and nothing more—

because of these, am I not to be allowed the rights — and the feelings that other girls have? No, I can't bear it. I will not have it, Falcon——'

Tears gushed from Mary's eyes, and an hysterical sob choked her voice. She waved her hand in an agitated manner, in sign that Falcon should leave her.

He bent on his knee at her feet, and kissed the hand with which she was dismissing him.

' Oh, my Queen!' he exclaimed passionately. ' It is because you are the girl—the woman, that I seem hard with you—because you are so adorable—because—— Oh, how can I explain? Mary, forgive me. Have patience with me.'

' I forgive you, General—if I have anything to forgive,' said Mary, recovering herself at the sight of his agitation. ' But I am tired and a little overdone, and I am weary of all this talk about playing parts and securing allies. Let me be for the present; and when I am enjoying the roses and the moonlight, and—and Don José's fun, don't frown upon me and poison all my harmless pleasure. It's only for a few days, General. Let me be happy for a few days.'

He left her ; and for the rest of that day was soft and tender in his manner as she could wish.

' I fancy " the zeal of your house has eaten him up," ' said Bellarmin.

He spoke of General Falcon, whose moody manner had been the subject of discussion ; if, indeed, that could be called discussion, in which Mary's part consisted only of constrained and embarrassed answers. They were walking alone together in the grounds of Stonehenge, and their footsteps had turned towards a little pine-forest, not far from the house, which was one of Mary's favourite resorts. Mary was grave, and seemed depressed. Bellarmin was grave, too. Sir Victor Champion was to arrive that day. He was concerned also on Mary's account. He feared that her poor little project would only break to pieces among all the schemes that were going on ; and he was daily growing to have more and more distrust of the discretion of General Falcon.

There was a little summer-house standing on the green moss just at the pine-wood's edge.

'Let us go in,' Mary said abruptly. 'I want to sit in that summer-house; it is of bark, and it reminds me of Karl August's summer-house of bark—that Goethe was so fond of—in the park at Weimar. Don't you remember?'

'No, I never was at Weimar.'

'How strange! Why don't you go at once?'

He did not particularly want to go anywhere at the time, away from the spot where they were standing.

'I am so busy with politics,' he said; 'I am tied to London.'

He spoke almost sullenly. He was a little vexed with her for dropping the subject of Falcon. She seemed to guess his thoughts, for she said, in a meditative but resolute manner, as she sat down on one of the bark seats:

'Yes, I know it. Indeed, I am afraid Falcon makes a conscience out of me. He compels himself to believe that whatever is of advantage to me is the right thing to do. I almost think I could make him run away from a battle if I could only appear at the critical moment and tell him that it would interfere with my plans if he did not instantly quit the field.   It is very serious having the soul of a grown man thus on one's conscience.'

'I have an instinctive impression that General Falcon doesn't like me,' Bellarmin said. 'I am sorry, for I wanted to like him. He hardly takes any pains to conceal his dislike.'

'Oh! that is it? He thinks you are too light and frivolous, I fancy,' Miss Beaton said, with an evident effort to seem unconcerned. 'And then I don't suppose he takes much to anyone who interests or amuses me.   He has not really any conscientious objection to my being amused ; but he thinks I ought to be amused in a more queenly sort of way.   I should not be surprised if he were to get it into his mind that you abet me in my frivolity instead of discouraging me.   But, pray, don't try to win his affections by joining with him to discourage me.   Life is in general a very melancholy piece of business, Mr. Bel-

larmin.   The sadness seems to peep out upon
us from all sides, as something gruesome
appears to do sometimes when we are walking in the dark—don't you know? And I think
we want every help to get us out of the gloom
and the morbidness as often as we can.   At
least, I find it so,' she said, with a half-
suppressed sigh.

' Yet surely life must have been very bright
and happy for you ?' Bellarmin said, in a tone
of the deepest interest.

' You think so ?   Why ?' said Mary, turning upon him with a sort of mournful
solemnity. ' Because my mother died when
I was only a child ; because my father died
when I was only a girl ; because I have no
kith or kin who are in any true way dear to
me ; because I have to live the life of a sham
Princess ; because I am surrounded by a tiny
mock Court ; because I have to do the things
I don't want to do, and can hardly ever do
any of the things I want to do ; because I
have always been walled about with forms
and ceremonies ; and because I know that I
am a centre of all manner of plans and
schemes which are not likely to come to any-

thing ; because I hardly ever knew any young people or could talk to other girls freely ; because—oh, a lot of other becauses, which I don't mean to run through ! If all this means happiness, then indeed, God-a-mercy, I am the very happiest young woman in England !'

Bellarmin was infinitely touched by her words, which seemed to him but the echo of some of his own thoughts. He was impressed, too, by the evidence of the clear good sense and reasonableness which her little speech contained. It broke down all the barriers of reserve he had set up within himself. ' Madame,' he said, with a certain diffidence and yet with impulsive earnestness, ' may I speak to you a little freely ? You will not take offence at what I say ?'

She fixed her deep, soft eyes on him. ' Yes ; say what you like, Mr. Bellarmin. I know you would not say anything which was meant to wound or to vex me. I am not a woman to take offence at the words of a friend.'

' It is this : why allow yourself to be employed in these visionary schemes ? Why keep chasing a phantom? You must have seen for yourself long ago that there is no chance, no hope, or even ghost of a chance. Why waste away the sweetest years of your life in an ambition which can come to nothing, and which I don't believe is your ambition at all?'

'And it is Mr. Bellarmin who speaks to me in this way,' she said, with a dreamy far-off look in her eyes; 'Mr. Bellarmin, of whom his friends and his enemies alike say that he is the most ambitious man in England!'

'Do they say that of me?' Bellarmin asked, with a shadow coming over his face. He would have wished her just then to think of him as made for something better than mere political ambition.

'Yes; they say that of you. They say that you threw in your fortunes with the Tory Party, because you thought there were much better chances for a man of talent or genius, or whatever it is, with the Tories than with the Liberals. See how I have learned your political gossip and your political vocabulary already! Yes; they do say that; and do you know, Mr. Bellarmin, I was rather attracted by it. It seemed interesting;

the idea of the young man thus letting his ambition go its own way. If I were a man, I should be in your House of Commons. It seems to me the only place left now where the honourable ambition of a man of spirit can find outlet or goal. And *you* preach to me against ambition !'

'I am not so ambitious as I was,' he said slowly ; 'at least, in the same sort of way. I think differently about some things ; I have altered my standard of value ; I shall perhaps alter it more and more. Besides, even if I were acting only out of mere ambition, it is an ambition which has clear, practical objects before it—objects that one might in reason hope to attain.'

'And mine has none such,' she said gravely. 'I understand what you mean. But you don't quite know what my secret ambition really was. Shall I tell you? From my childhood up, those around me kept telling me I was like Mary Stuart. Well, it became my pride to be like her ; my one ambition to be more and more like her. Yes ; you can't know, you *couldn't* know, how this ambition filled my soul, and governed almost every movement I made. To be like Mary Stuart; to captivate hearts of women as well as men, just as she did; to be a great politician like her—even to go to the scaffold like her—that was my dream. It was charming enough over there, when one was a sort of star of a small Court, and had nobody near but those who flattered one's vanity, and taught one to believe in one's self. But here—well, one learns a different lesson. It is like coming straight from the dream of the morning into the cold, hard life of a London street, where you are jostled by a whole crowd, and known by nobody. My dream is over.'

As she stood up, and let her hands fall by her sides with the gesture of one who dismisses an illusion for ever, she looked more like Mary Stuart than she had ever seemed to Bellarmin before. His soul was filled with sympathy, with pity, with intense admiration.

'From that dream,' he said softly, 'who could wish to rouse you? Not I, at least. But the other illusion, why encourage it; why keep it up? It can only end in the most utter disappointment; even, perhaps, disaster.'

She turned upon him vehemently, passionately.

'What would you have me do?' she
asked.

'Live here in England and be happy,
since you like the place. Give up all the
appearance and the retinue of a Court—the
sham royalty; drop the part of exiled Princess—you don't seem to like it, or to believe
in it any more than I do; meet society as an
Englishwoman, as the daughter of an English
peer—as what you are. You will find in
English life all you want—all that even am-
·bition can want; and you will have the sense
of being real.'

She smiled, a rather wan and melancholy
smile.

'Yes, they are right, Mr. Bellarmin. You
are an ambitious man. Perhaps all men are
like that in one way or other. Don't you
notice that you have not appealed to me by
one single word which did not concern my
personal ambition or my personal feelings of
some kind? Why did you not tell me that
if I settled down to the quiet life of a London
lady I might have plenty of opportunities of

doing some good for the poor and the miserable, about whom you have so often heard me lamenting ? I suppose you suspected that there was nothing very deep and lasting in the tone of the lamentation—that it was of the same order of sentiment as my sham Mary Stuartism, and my sham pretensions to the place of a princess. But, do you know, I think you were wrong—I think you judged me wrongly. I think if anyone could show me how I could better serve some unhappy human creatures, I might be glad to give up my life and my claims and my aerial royalty, and to live and die a benevolent old maid! There—I have been talking enough about myself, and enough of nonsense—for once ; and see, Mr. Bellarmin, there is Sir Victor Champion.'

The statesman was coming towards them in the company of Lord Stonehenge and Monsignor Valmy. He was deep in conversation with the priest, and his fine intellectual head, with its clear-cut features and rather long hair, was bent in grave interest. Both Mary and Bellarmin noted the firm elastic manner of his tread, his look of force and vitality, and the dominance which his whole bearing suggested.

' He is a great man,' said the girl, almost below her breath.

' Yes, he is a great man,' Bellarmin answered.

Sir Victor's face lighted with pleasure—and something more than pleasure—at the sight of Mary Beaton. His manner of greeting her was peculiar. He took her two hands in his as a fatherly old friend might have done, but he bowed over them with all the deference of a courtier.

CHAPTER V.

THE STONEHENGE NEGOTIATIONS.

IT was perfectly well understood at Stonehenge that Sir Victor Champion was to be pleased and conciliated. Nobody said this; nobody distinctly gave it out; certainly neither Lord Stonehenge nor Monsignor Valmy uttered a word on the subject to the general company; but the purpose was afloat all the same. The nearest approach to any open allusion to this policy was made one morning by Stonehenge to Monsignor Valmy in one of the libraries— the house had several libraries.

'How does one best please a great man?' Stonehenge asked, as if abstractedly.

' By making him think he is pleasing everybody,' was the ready and quiet answer.

Stonehenge smiled.

' I believe you are right,' he said ; ' but are there not great men who don't care to please ?'

' I never met one. Great men, like small men, get sour and rough when they think they have not the art of pleasing. A man must care for men before he can become a misanthrope.'

Everyone, according to Horace, drags his tail. Everyone, according to the American politician's expression, has his axe to grind. There was some silent preparation for the grinding of axes at Stonehenge. Lord Stonehenge's icy integrity of purpose did not in the least interfere to keep him out of this general grinding operation. He was one of the men who will readily do, for a cause, things which they would disdain to do for themselves. He was therefore willing to go out of his way to conciliate Champion, and even to conciliate Bellarmin, for the sake of Mary Beaton's claims. The money claims are, of course, understood ; Lord Stonehenge knew far more about Mary Beaton's pecuniary affairs than she did herself, and knew that her suspicion was correct ; and he knew that Falcon was playing a venturesome game, and that if the money claims on the British Government were not soon acknowledged, the poor Princess's Court and state dignity, such as they were, must all too soon contract, or even collapse. He was fully convinced of the moral and even the legal justice of the claims, but he knew they would stand in need of vigorous and clever Parliamentary pushing. A man like Bellarmin might be very useful ; but a man like Sir Victor Champion would be invaluable.

Monsignor Valmy was of the same mind as Lord Stonehenge, and was prepared to assist him in his projects ; but the priest's motives were not quite the same as those of his host. Monsignor Valmy was particularly anxious that Lord Stonehenge should marry. It was about time, he thought. Stonehenge was no longer young ; Stonehenge's brother, who would succeed in the event of the elder having no son, was a good-for-nothing creature, a purposeless idler, and a man about town. Therefore Monsignor Valmy wanted Stonehenge to marry, and the dearest wish of his heart on that subject was that Stonehenge should marry Mary Beaton.

Sir Victor Champion came to Stonehenge Park very much because Mary Beaton had attracted him, and he wished to see more of her, but principally to have the opportunity of talking over Bellarmin. Bellarmin came to meet Mary Beaton because she had bidden him ; not because he intended to be false to Lady Saxon's claim upon him—but perhaps because his conscience revolted against that claim, and Mary's influence was like a soothing anodyne. Mary had come to be amused, and she found, alas ! that amusement was not precisely the object she had attained. She did not analyze her feelings, however, but allowed herself to drift as the current bore her. And Bellarmin did the same ; and he relaxed his guard upon himself and allowed his scruples to be lulled under the sweet charm of her society.

So these two young people grew into closer intimacy and companionship ; and almost unconsciously to both, neither of them looked forward with any great eagerness to Sir Victor's arrival. It seemed to Mary, somehow, that the best part of her holiday would be over; and Bellarmin found reason to believe, from what Mary had said to him, that Sir Victor would try to make a political convert of him. Lady Saxon had prepared him for this too; and he remembered his promise to her, and faithfully intended to keep it. But she had not given him to understand that Champion would go out of his way to make immediate overtures. The idea was a little embarrassing, but he could not run away. Indeed, he had no wish to run away, and he was only made uncomfortable by his own attitude of uncertainty and Sir Victor's coolness. Nor was his discomfort in any way diminished by the manner in which Sir Victor devoted himself to Mary, and the increasing gratification which—he told his vexed heart—Mary was learning to feel from the great statesman's attentions.

Certainly Sir Victor Champion was very much attracted by Mary Stuart Beaton; and certainly also no one suspected the true nature of the attraction less than Mary herself. Falcon observed it, and grew more and more silent and sullen ; and Bellarmin noticed it and was jealous, though he told himself that he had no right to care ; and Stonehenge saw it, and his manner to Sir Victor became even more courteous, and his manner to Mary even more gentle and friendly still. But the sadness in his refined face deepened ; and there seemed in it a yet greater likeness to his melancholy-featured ancestor who had given up his life for the King at Newbury.

To Mary, and even contrary to her expectations, Sir Victor's presence was a relief and a pleasure. She was a little wayward, this girl, and there had come upon her a vague reaction, after her innocent flirtation with Bellarmin. She felt so safe with Sir Victor, who was so much older than the rest, not very much younger indeed than Falcon ; for what difference is there between a man of forty-seven and a man of sixty-five in the eyes of a girl of twenty ? And then the man who would be Prime Minister of England was upon a plane far removed from that occupied by the others. It did not occur to her

that he might be looked upon as a possible
suitor. She need not stand upon ceremony
with him, or have any fear of giving cause for
misconstruction. His great gifts and his important position in the service of his country,
justified her in granting him privileges to
which even Falcon could not object. In this
regard, she had the pleasing consciousness
that she was fulfilling Falcon's behests, and
that in a way that was perfectly natural to her.
She had got over her first little shyness with
him. She even presumed sometimes to make
a jest of his political prospects. 'When you
are Prime Minister and busy abolishing the
House of Lords, you won't have time to explain the British Constitution to me,' she
would say laughingly. But in the meanwhile
she begged him to tell her all about the Constitution and about many other matters besides ; and she would listen to him with the
deepest attention, and would ask him sudden
naïve questions about the English Court and
about the business of statecraft, and about the
great measures he had helped to make law.
Sometimes, too, they would talk seriously about
legislation and the amelioration of national

evils ; and he would listen to her ignorant criticisms on life, which were withal so fresh to him, and encourage her to give out to him her crude enthusiasms with an interest and indulgence which would have made some of his political followers, anxious to get the ear of their chief for their own particular theories, turn pale with wrath and envy. Thus Mary found a constant and delightful companion in Sir Victor, and was innocently flattered by his attentions. She had perhaps visions of doing good, and of exercising a beneficent political influence ; and she had already made him promise to go with her to visit her South-wark parish, that he might see for himself the poverty and the misery which she fancied he had never had time to look into ; and he was going to help her in emigrating some of the starving artisans ; and he was going to give consideration to the feasibility of providing food for the children who came breakfastless to the Board schools, and went home with little prospect of a dinner. All this so filled her mind, that she almost forgot the Stuart claims and the part she was expected to fulfil. Had she remembered, she might

not have succeeded in playing her part so
well.

There was a certain strain of mysticism and
of veneration in Champion's nature that struck
a chord harmonious with that devotional
tendency so marked in Mary Beaton, and
which was perhaps an hereditary trait in her.
To Sir Victor, the society of the priests was
a source of peculiar pleasure. He liked to
lead up to philosophical and metaphysical discussion, to talk of the development of creeds,
to compare rather than to contrast the doc-
trines of schools, to endeavour to enter into
the feelings of the worshipper of Pasht, and
the self-suppression of the hermit in the
Thebaid. Materialism was the only form of
human belief or disbelief into which Champion
found himself absolutely incapable of entering,
which had for him no meaning, and won from
him no sympathy. Monsignor Valmy also
delighted in such subjects of discussion, and
Champion found something strangely congenial in the strain of spiritual idealism which
the ecclesiastic infused into his conversation.
Monsignor Valmy's Catholicism was of the
widest range ; to one not of his own faith he

rarely talked of creed, save in its most abstract sense. Men not of his own faith sometimes found fault with his very wideness of view and his comprehensive, candid tolerance of differing opinion. It was the arrogance of the Roman churchman, they would have it; he was so satisfied of the final triumph of his own Church, that he already regarded every other human creature as one of the same fold, whether the other human creature would have it so or not. The gentle resignation and sweet piety of Dr. Amblaine had, on the other hand, a soothing effect on the mind of the world-fretted statesman, and helped him the more to enjoy his holiday at Stonehenge. It was one of the peculiarities of Champion's complex nature that, iconoclast as he was supposed to be, iconoclast as indeed in one sense he was, his soul was suffused with the sentiment of reverence and religion.

One day Monsignor Valmy touched delicately on this seeming contradiction.

'It sounds strangely in my ears, Sir Victor,' he said, 'when I hear people talk of you as a man of revolutionary ideas. I always think of you as, in spirit, one of *us*—of us who believe in the guiding Hand from above, in faith founded at the beginning of things, and in the Divine order of the universe.'

' I understand you,' Champion said musingly ; ' I confess it is a thing by which my own mind has sometimes been vaguely puzzled. But you will not think me arrogant when I say that I believe the destroyer of the form is often he who is most profoundly reverent of the spirit. Would you not admit that something of the kind might be said of Pascal ?—not that I am vain enough to compare myself with Pascal. It is the tendency of our progress, or what we call progress, to thicken and increase the outer layers which envelop the soul of a national or a religious institution, so that the inner light shows more and more dimly, until at last it ceases, to most eyes, to be visible at all. Then is the time for the reformer to rend and tear away ; and while he is doing this, he seems no doubt to be putting the light out, but his only object is to let it blaze forth to the world again in all its pure and pristine brilliancy. I hold,' he went on after a brief silence, during which the priest's eyes had been steadfastly fixed on his face—'I hold that the reformer is as much the product of previous causes and effects as the very condition of things it is his mission to destroy. He is but an instrument, and has no power of controlling the tendencies and the sometimes contradictory impulses which guide him this way or that, but always to a certain goal—unrecognised, it may be, even by himself. What seems a stupendous egotism may be but instinctive submission to a compelling destiny.'

'Yes,' answered Monsignor Valmy. 'Amid all our philosophies and attempts at solution of the many problems of life, it seems inevitable that the soul should fall back upon the idea of the Hebraistic God—the personal ruling divinity.'

'You are right,' said Champion. 'It is a strange feeling,' he went on thoughtfully, his dark eyes dilating as they always did in moments of earnestness, ' to find one's self, after having tried to worship the Pantheistic God, as all with the artistic temperament are sure to do, in touch once more with the Hebraistic Deity of our childhood. Wasn't it Heine who said at the last, " The Pantheistic God is of no use " ? One is forced, as you say, to submit to the idea of a celestial despotism—the edict given forth from above —and to the practice of a blind faith. The worst of it is, a horrible doubt whether our drafts of faith will be honoured. It does sometimes seem, in our disheartened moods, as though the Demiourgos had been permitted to make a world and were laughing at his own experiment; and it is this kind of mood, Monsignor Valmy, that the Church and its discipline alone can combat successfully.'

'We have the law from above and the interpreter here below,' replied Valmy. 'It is often said that the discipline of the Church exercises a stultifying effect upon man's will. Not so ; the object of discipline is to train and purify and eventually free the will, so that it becomes, in a sense, a separate entity. Sorrow, struggle, and experience are needed for this ; and the spiritual education that the Church gives may be more rapid and effectual than that wrought through the illusions of life. Face to face with love and death— either in spirit or body—the Pantheistic God vanishes.' As he uttered the word 'love,' a certain far-off human emotion seemed to light the priest's thin ascetic countenance. He looked dreamily towards Bellarmin as he spoke. 'What support is there in flower or sunset, in forest glory or beauty of trackless sea, to the soul fighting in the open? "My God, my God, why hast Thou forsaken me?" becomes its natural utterance in the hour of crisis.'

'What puzzles me most,' broke in Rolfe Bellarmin, who had come nearer during the discussion—'what puzzles me most in the method of humanity's government, is that process of education by illusion. It makes us sceptics at one stage or another. We go through so many phases that sometimes it is impossible to believe in the reality of any of our emotions. That's the most hurtful sort of scepticism, I think, and the most likely to make us feel that everything is chance, or that a devil has the management of affairs. Seems an odd form of education, don't it, which creates distrust in the whole scheme? I have sometimes got hold of a notion that our bodies are taken possession of now and then by wandering spirits, and that we die and are born again many times in our lives. One looks back upon a love that is dead, a condition of mind that has completely altered, an enthusiasm that has vanished to the winds, and the remembrance of which only provokes a smile ; and though there runs a certain slight thread of continuity through all, the man who passed through each of these stages is, without doubt, a different I.'

Bellarmin spoke with bitterness. He was thinking of experiences of his own.

'Ah!' began Mary Beaton impetuously ; ' I, too, have felt the same.'

She had come nearer also. It sometimes seemed as though Champion unconsciously exercised a sort of magnetic influence, so that when he talked, those who were a little apart dropped their own conversation and drew towards him. The girl glanced at Bellarmin with quickened interest. They had been sitting together, and their talk had touched upon one subject after another in a vague, fugitive manner till, a little while before, they had subsided into silence. It was a rainy afternoon, and several of the party had collected in the vast hall, which was large enough for each one to pursue his or her separate avocation quite alone and apart if so inclined. The sound of falling drops on the glass dome overhead, the subdued light entering through stained windows, the oak-panelled walls and massive carved mantels, the dim faces of the portraits, the spectral suits of armour, and, indeed, the whole atmosphere of the place, produced a dreamy sense of languor, and a not disagreeable melancholy that was conducive to such a tone of conversation.

' I don't believe that we *are* ourselves,' the girl went on, in an eager tone; ' I mean that I half believe in the theory that we have all lived before, and that everything we do and think and say is just carrying on what we were in some former life—like a flower that springs up again when summer comes, the same that it was last summer, only that it is another flower.'

' A new rose on the old stem,' said Monsignor Valmy, smiling indulgently upon her.

' Monsignor,' said Mary, turning to him in a reverential manner, ' I hope that you do not find anything heretical in my fanciful idea, which, after all, is so old and so much in people's minds nowadays.'

'The bosom of our Mother Church is great enough surely, and tender enough, to enfold all theories which, in darker ages, have brought troubled humanity nearer to the Divine Ruler,' replied Monsignor gravely. 'I have never thought of the theory of re-incarnation as totally opposed to the Divine revelation which we have received. It would, on the contrary, seem to throw some light upon difficult problems with which, however, we need not greatly concern ourselves, seeing that God has given us faith and light for our guidance in this present life, and the assurance of a most blessed spiritual condition when it is ended.'

The priest leaned back in his chair, and his eyes were lowered to the cross on his breast, as he were silently communing with his soul. There was a little pause. Presently Champion said, glancing from Miss Beaton's face to the portrait of Mary Stuart which hung near to where she was sitting, 'Madame's theory might certainly gain corroboration from that picture, and would open out a field of very romantic speculation.'

'At least,' said Stonehenge, who had come

in a few moments before, 'it would go towards explaining that curious thread of destiny which seems to run through all human relationships, and which draws certain groups of persons together. Has it ever struck you, considering the inexhaustible capabilities of life, how limited is the sphere of each of us, and how, in spite of continual efforts that some of us make to change surrounding conditions, we are impelled by persons, associations, tendencies—all sorts of intangible but irresistible influences—to follow a course perhaps entirely opposed to our wishes and inclinations ?'

'In fact,' said Champion, 'every group represents a psychological drama, for the *dénoûment* of which we can only wait.' Then he branched off abruptly to discussion of the Greek Fate, and its influence upon later drama. 'Fate works on groups,' he said ; ' never on one sole human being. Man is never alone with Fate ; the Greeks understood this.'

Shut off from the outside world though they were, the little party found no lack of interest and amusement. A week passed very quickly amid such surroundings as those of Stonehenge Park. They did not go out on the lake again after dinner; but it was discovered that the Reverend Dr. Amblaine had a passion for the violoncello almost equal to that with which he cherished his books, and that Champion added to his varied gifts a fine cultivated taste in music. So there were concerts every evening within doors. The Prince of Saragossa and Miss Beaton sang duets to the accompaniment of piano and violoncello; Lady Struthers performing on the former instrument, and the two young people representing an operatic scena in dramatic fashion. Then Mary's sweet, clear voice would sometimes break into a Border song or a melancholy Scotch ballad, and Champion himself was more than once caught joining in a spirited Jacobite chorus. Sometimes Bellarmin would steal out through the open window into the night, and from the shelter of a trellis of roses he would gaze into the lighted room and upon the fair face of Mary Stuart Beaton, as she stood by the piano, with her bosom gently heaving under the stiff brocaded bodice, and her soft brown eyes upraised and alight, and all her heart in the pathetic words of the well-known song which thrilled her listeners :

> ‘Yest’r-e’en the Queen had four Maries,
>   The day she’ll hae but three :
> There was Mary Beaton, and Mary Seton,
>   And Mary Carmichael, and me.’

It was a mournful plaint, and the young girl's voice trembled with genuine emotion when she reached the last verse.

Somehow it hurt Bellarmin that anything so tragic should be associated with his bright, winsome Mary. The same thought must have been in Champion's mind, for he went up to her when she had ended, and said with affectionate insistence :

‘ Oh, do not sing that again while we are here ! Do me this great favour. The feeling you put into it is too real. *You* ought to awaken only joyous memories. *Our* Mary Stuart shall recall no darksome suggestion of Holyrood. The brightness and the bloom shall be hers. Let the tragedy remain in the past.’

Notwithstanding his earlier designs, it is possible that Sir Victor was so much engrossed with Mary Beaton's society as to be willing to let all vulgar worldly considerations go by for the moment. Or, perhaps, with a certain Epicurean thoroughness, which characterized his temperament where his pleasures were concerned, he wished to enjoy to the full the idyllic charm of this country visit without too hastily introducing a discordant element. It was enough to talk ecclesiasticism with Monsignor Valmy, literature with Stonehenge and Dr. Amblaine, abstract Jacobitism with Falcon, and to explore the recesses of Mary's intelligent mind without bringing practical politics to the fore—at any rate, for a day or two. However that might have been, he did not rush at Bellarmin. He was extremely courteous and friendly to the young man, but nothing in his manner showed any desire for a private conference. Bellarmin began to think that Miss Beaton must have been mistaken, and that no purpose beyond that of enlisting Champion's sympathy in the question of the Stuart inheritance had been in anyone's mind. Perhaps he was, after all, just a little disappointed. He was not, then, so important a personage as people imagined.

Some two or three mornings after Sir

Victor's arrival, Bellarmin was standing on the terrace looking vaguely over the trees and the lake and the whole landscape. He was moody and discontented, though he hardly dared to analyze his feelings; and he was beginning to be conscious of an uncomfortable questioning within himself as to why, having obeyed Miss Beaton's command and come to Stonehenge Park, he now remained there, when he did not seem to be much wanted. The whole of that morning he had not seen Mary. She did not seem inclined to visit the summer-house now. 'She is better occupied,' he said to himself; and then came the murmur, 'I think I'll go back to London.'

'This is better than London, Mr. Bellarmin,' a rich and musical voice said at his very ear. Bellarmin almost started. The words sounded so like an answer to his thought, that for a moment he doubted whether he had not expressed his thought aloud. But Sir Victor Champion, who had come out of the house and was standing beside him, was evidently offering a general observation. So Bellarmin agreed that the terrace at Stonehenge was a better place on which to pass a fine morning than even the terrace of the House of Commons.

'You know the history of this place, no doubt,' Sir Victor said carelessly ; 'Lord Stonehenge would have told you.'

'I have a rough general idea,' Bellarmin answered, not feeling quite sure whether Sir Victor really wanted to talk about Stonehenge Park or not ; 'I haven't had much chance of hearing Lord Stonehenge talk about it.'

'Not yet ? No ? Well, it is one of the most delightful narratives in the history of our great family houses. I am satisfied that no country is so rich as England in the history of houses—family houses. But I must not anticipate Lord Stonehenge's description. He can show you everything—the exact spot of which each tradition speaks. Get him to show you. He will like to be asked. He is shy. He wants to be made to talk—to be drawn out.'

'I shall be delighted to hear something about it from you, meanwhile, Sir Victor. I am sure you know all about it just as well as Lord Stonehenge.'

'No, no.   It would be unfair—in a man's own house.   Besides, as I have got hold of you, Mr. Bellarmin, I think I should rather talk to you about something else—just now.'

'My time is come,' Bellarmin said to himself.   Aloud he said, 'Anything you wish, Sir Victor.'

'Suppose we walk up and down, Mr. Bellarmin.   A little chilly still, don't you think so?'

Bellarmin remembered Osric's way of falling in with the Lord Hamlet's changes of mood concerning the weather.   But he said nothing on that subject, and the twain began to pace up and down the great terrace.

'We are the only two politicians in this house at present,' Sir Victor said, 'you and I. One can hardly call Lord Stonehenge a politician—he lives in a more rarefied atmosphere than that of politics; although I, for one, have not admitted that a politician may not breathe the very purest air.'

'When are we coming to the point?' Bellarmin asked himself; 'when are we to hear of the new political combination?' Sir Victor apparently was not coming to it at all, for he only said :

' I have observed your Parliamentary career with great interest, Mr. Bellarmin. You seem instinctively to have gone the right way about it. A young man now must seize the attention of the House of Commons if he wants to get a chance within any reasonable time. It was different in my early Parliamentary days. Then, we young men were supposed to be bound down by all sorts of forms and rules not to open our mouths until the middle of our second session, and so on. All that was absurd. I believe in young men, and the fresh breath coming in from the outer world.'

There was a subtle suggestion in all this that Bellarmin's early escapades in the House of Commons were the outcome of deliberate purpose and keen Parliamentary foresight. Bellarmin was pleased, but he felt that he could not accept the praise with a clear conscience.

' I am afraid that it was schoolboy impetuosity, Sir Victor, and not any reasonable purpose.'

' No, no. I am sure you do yourself injustice. It only amounts to this, that you came in under new conditions, and you saw—instinctively perhaps—that there were new conditions, and what they were. I have observed other young men who came in about the same time as you, and if you will excuse me for saying so, under more favouring auspices—such as the traditional influence of great families, and all that—and they are yet waiting to begin, while you have already —well, made a name.'

Bellarmin could not but feel gratified. Sir Victor's words sounded genuine.

'Of course you have yet to make your way,' Sir Victor went on. ' But you will do that. The quick judgment which has guided you so far will guide you still farther. You have not been speaking quite so often of late. That, too, is well—in a young man who wants to show that he can be something more than a young man. You were right at first, and you are right now.'

' I fear I only followed my humour in both instances,' Bellarmin said, with a boyish smile. At first Bellarmin had felt somewhat as a snake might have felt when about to be

brought within the sphere of the serpent-
charmer. He fancied that he was, in a sort
of way, entrapped into the magic circle, and
that he would need to have all his faculties at
work if he would escape with his freedom.
But as he got into easy talk with Sir Victor, he
found this sensation began to fade, and he felt
with each instant less and less necessity for
keeping on his guard. Sir Victor did not seem
to be greatly interested in any partizan plots or
schemings. He appeared only to be occupied
with a kind of professional or artistic interest
in the Parliamentary career of Bellarmin himself. He spoke as the veteran general of
division might talk, when in sympathetic
mood and in the sheltered familiarity of private intercourse, to the promising young
cadet whom he has already seen more than
once under fire.

'Well, yes; I said that you had got into
the right way instinctively; but in all such
cases what we call instinct is only unconscious
intellectual foresight. You began, of course,
where I began—where we all begin. Strange
what a fascination for young Englishmen that
conservative principle has! There is some-

thing romantic and poetic about it, I suppose.
One venerates it—like an old English ruin
with the ivy clinging round it.'

' Must one cease to venerate the ruin, Sir
Victor ?'

' Oh no ; I hope not—surely not ; but one
finds he can't live in the ruin and make it his
home. I found that. You are finding it. I
should not hasten my discovery if I were you,
or my disillusion, or whatever it is. It will
come in time. Let it wait.'

' People say you would like to rush things,
Sir Victor, don't they ?'

' Do they ? Yes ; I suppose they do. But
that is quite a mistake. The only foundation
for it is that I like to have the country prepared for a change that is inevitable. To go
back to our ruin—when I see some of the
walls of the house beginning to crumble, I
think it well to set about arranging for re-
building or removal. I don't believe it wise
policy to wait till the roof comes crashing in.
That is my idea about the House of Lords.'

Sir Victor looked Bellarmin frankly in the
face. There was frankness, more than frankness—there was an implied fulness of con-

fidence in the words and the look. The plans about the House of Lords were supposed to be so entirely confidential between Champion and his closest political agents, that any agent who made the very disclosure he was sent out to make might be repudiated by his chief. This had been put very plainly to Bellarmin by the unabashed Tressel. Bellarmin was therefore all the more surprised to hear Sir Victor now refer so openly and directly to his policy about the House of Lords. It could only be a compliment to Bellarmin. Bellarmin accepted it accordingly.

'You see you have raised the question yourself,' Sir Victor said, with a good-natured smile. 'You were thinking about the House of Lords, of course, when you spoke of what people were saying of me, and my desire to rush things.'

'I am afraid I was thinking of that,' Bellarmin answered, a little angry with himself for having given Sir Victor his chance so easily, and a good deal amused too.

'Yes; why not? I am not at all sorry that you have come to the question so frankly and directly.'

'Did I come to the question frankly and directly?' Bellarmin asked.

'As you have touched upon it, I may say that I am rather glad to have a chance of saying a word or two, in the way of explanation, perhaps.'

Bellarmin bowed. He did not want to commit himself too rashly again.

'You must understand that I had no idea, or hope, or wish even, to induce you to separate yourself from your party at such a stage of the question. You understand that?'

'I was not quite certain,' Bellarmin answered rather coldly; 'it was all somewhat vague.'

'Vague? Oh no! I wanted to give your party—your friends—a fair chance. I wanted them to do nothing more than simply say they don't pledge themselves to oppose all reform in that direction. But I don't suppose they will do even that.'

'Oh, surely, yes,' Bellarmin said hastily. 'No man in his senses goes in for finality in politics now.'

'They will say they do, I am afraid, in that.'

'They may refuse to say anything, at some particular moment, on some sudden demand. That I could quite understand. No one has a right to make a sudden call on a great party for a declaration of policy on some question which has not yet come up.' Bellarmin spoke warmly now.

'Of course not; such a demand would be unreasonable, and your friends would be quite warranted in refusing to answer it. But they won't be content with that, Mr. Bellarmin. You will find it before long. Your leaders will pledge the party to what they will call an absolute, final, and irrevocable decision.'

'It can't be; it is impossible. They would have consulted me,' he was going to say, but he checked himself. 'They would have consulted all of us.'

'They certainly ought to have consulted *you*. I was quite willing and anxious, as you know. They do not seem to have thought it necessary. But they have made up their minds all the same.'

'Made up their minds!—about what, Sir Victor?'

Sir Victor looked at him with a benevolent,

or even a compassionate smile. 'I see they have not taken you into their confidence,' he said. 'Well, Mr. Bellarmin, it is just this. Their leaders had the opportunity, the full opportunity, of consulting and co-operating with me as to the course which a scheme of reform in that direction ought to take, and they rejected it—positively and finally rejected it. I see you are surprised at this, and I don't wonder at your surprise. I own I was a little astonished myself, although I didn't expect much. Well, we can talk about this another time, if we haven't talked about it enough already.'

Bellarmin felt touched to the very quick. Sir Victor had put the thrust home. So then his own party, his own leaders, had been acting without him, had never consulted him— never, apparently, thought him worth consulting ; and all the time he had been fancying himself a sort of leader, an ally, at least, who must be thought of and consulted at any crisis. Could it be true ? It must be true. Champion was up to many political crafts and Parliamentary arts ; but no one had ever accused him of a readiness to say the thing which was not. It must be true; and this, then, was the return for all the bold service he had rendered, the risks he had run, the chances he had deliberately thrown away! Sir Victor Champion had thought him worth consulting, and he had held back and refused; and this was his reward. The young man's heart burned within him. He was in the Coriolanus mood.

'The truth is—I believe—I am told,' Sir Victor said hesitatingly, 'they don't quite appreciate anything original and brilliant, especially anything humorous.'

Bellarmin could not help thinking that people generally said that Sir Victor himself was sadly lacking in appreciation of the humorous. But that was not a matter quite to the point just then.

'Surely De Carmel,' he said, naming the brilliant Tory leader, once the light of the Commons, then a funeral lamp in the Lords, now extinguished altogether—'surely De Carmel was not of that way of thinking?'

'Ah, De Carmel? Well, no; not he. De Carmel, of course, was a sort of Bohemian, a sort of Zingaro; he had a sort of Maugrabin art and humour of his own.   I never thought very highly of it myself—not very highly. But even he, when he got into the Lords, became so different.   He always seemed to feel that, after all, he was only an outsider— that he didn't belong to the place ; he had to be very respectable, and to go in specially for consulting all the proprieties and the conventionalities.   Like Miss Fotheringay, you know, when she got elevated into Lady Mirabel—you remember—Pendennis ?'

Yes ; Bellarmin quite remembered.

' It was something like that with De Carmel in the Lords.   Besides, he was absolutely in the leading-strings of Lord Bosworth ; and Bosworth lately became quite determined, they tell me, that the party was to be altogether respectable in its action, and that eccentricity of any kind must be resolutely discouraged.   So De Carmel, who made the party by his eccentricity—what a man like Bosworth would call eccentricity, Mr. Bellarmin—what you and I would call originality, brilliancy, boldness, spirit—and so even De Carmel had to conform himself.   Very absurd ; but why did a man like him ever consent to swamp and submerge himself in a dull marsh like that ?' Sir Victor asked quite angrily.

Bellarmin was not thinking much just then about De Carmel's reasons for consenting to be transferred to the House of Lords.   He was thinking of Champion's words about himself.   Could it be possible, then, that the leaders of the party to which he had attached himself and had devoted himself looked upon him only as a sort of *gamin*, whose freaks were to be tolerated when his party was in Opposition, because such freaks annoyed and thwarted the men in office, but were to be repudiated the moment the Opposition had, and partly by his means, been transformed into an Administration ?   And could it be that he, who had always gone in for the right and duty of Conservatism to move abreast with the best movements of the age, was to be pledged by his leaders to a policy of stupid and impossible finality, no consent or concurrence of his being given or even being asked ?   Bellarmin would gladly have persuaded himself that his strongest feeling of dissatisfaction was on public grounds.

' They will wreck the party,' he said to himself grimly.

' Well, you will find that your leaders are pledged to finality,' Sir Victor said with a smile, 'and that they have pledged you too. I can't offer them another chance. I see, by the way, that Tressel has a motion down about the House of Lords. I don't know whether he means to bring it on. He is an odd sort of person, Tressel, as you know. One can't pretend to control him. If he should bring it on, that might give them an opportunity of qualifying in some way what I understood to be their decision. But I don't believe they will qualify it. Bosworth is master for the present. Well, I shan't move until the right time. Of course you will understand that this little morning talk of ours is entirely between ourselves ? Ah ! here comes Lord Stonehenge. Get him to tell you all about this place.'

Sir Victor left Bellarmin, and presently attached himself to Monsignor Valmy, to whom he poured forth a dissertation on the inner discipline of the order of the Jesuits. Monsignor Valmy listened with a bland sweet smile.

CHAPTER VI.

PETREL'S REST.

A MYSTERIOUS note was brought to General Falcon one morning, just before the break up of the Stonehenge party. The messenger had orders to wait. The note was addressed in a bold slanting hand. It was sealed and impressed with a curiously twisted monogram, and ran thus :

' Petrel's Rest, *June* ——.

' The bearer of this will have a carriage at the Stonehenge Arms, in which you can be brought here at once. I want particularly to see you ; and I don't want any fuss made about my sending for you, or about my presence in this neighbourhood, though there is

28—2

no reason why the fact shouldn't be chronicled in the county newspapers.

'J. S.'

Falcon sent a message to the effect that he would be at the Stonehenge Arms in half an hour. He made a short cut through the park, and was at the lodge gates soon after the bearer of the missive had passed through. He found a quiet-looking dog-cart standing in front of the inn, with a foreign servant beside it. The man touched his hat, and asked in German if he were the gentleman going to Petrel's Rest. Falcon got into the vehicle, and was driven at a rapid trot along the lanes in the direction of the sea.

The country about Stonehenge Park was well wooded and garden-like, with here and there a patch of pine-forest, which gave variety and picturesqueness to the landscape. Nearer the coast it grew wilder and more barren-looking—bleak downs and wastes of moorland, with scarcely any sign of habitation, rising gradually; and then an abrupt dip, as if a sort of natural rampart guarded the jagged fringe of land, which, with its beetling cliffs,

its hidden gulfs and inlets, and its rugged for-
bidding appearance, suggested thoughts of
mediæval romance, and tales of smuggling
and piracy, and dark and dangerous deeds.

Nothing could have been more isolated
than the situation of Petrel's Rest. It was
four miles from the nearest railway-station,
and there was scarcely a hamlet or even a
cottage within sight of it. The little tongue
of land upon which it was built jutted out in
the centre of a gloomy bay, closed in by lofty
promontories that terminated in bold precipices
of black rock. From the moorland, one seemed
to look down upon the gray beacon-like tower,
the foundations of which were washed on three
sides by the waters of the bay; but after
passing through the belt of pine-wood that
stretched from the downs to the very gates of
the place, it was difficult to believe that the
country at the back was in reality higher—the
cliff seemed so like a mountain crag, the still
bay with its rocky walls so like a lake; while
the descent from the tower platform was so
perpendicular, that without going to the very
edge of the terrace it was almost impossible
to realize that the sea lay so close below.

The castle had evidently been fortified at one period of its history.   Part of it had fallen into ruin ; and, indeed, the square tower and a small wing of more modern date, built on at the back, seemed the only portions fit for habitation.   It stood in a kind of courtyard, with great iron gates and a stone archway carved with armorial bearings.   The gates stood open now, but one could well fancy the clang with which they might close upon some hapless prisoner or little band of armed desperadoes.   The place seemed a survival of feudal times, and in its grayness, its look of age, its fortress-like simplicity, seemed so strangely out of keeping as a background with the personality of Lady Saxon—brilliant, modern, meretricious—that Falcon was set wondering and speculating upon the motive which induced her at times to seclude herself in so impregnable an eyry.   ‘She does not bring her husband here with her,’ he said to himself, with a grim smile.   ‘I should like to know who has been given the key of those rusty gates.’

He was admitted by another foreign servant, an elderly man, whose face seemed familiar to the eyes of the old General. It was Falcon's boast that he never forgot the countenance of any man or woman with whom he had once conversed for ten minutes.

'I think that I've seen you before,' he said. 'You used to receive Doctor Langenwelt's patients?'

'I was in the service of the late Baron Langenwelt,' replied the man, bowing.

General Falcon began to understand that Lady Saxon might find it convenient to employ foreign servants in this residence of hers, and especially servants who had known her as Madame Langenwelt. Doubtless they were well paid.

He followed the butler through a dim hall lined with tapestry, and in which a fire of pine-wood burned brightly, and into a sort of boudoir, where it was evident from the gorgeous colouring, the heavy Eastern carpets, the magnificent hangings, the luxurious divans, and fantastic Parisian knick-knacks, that Lady Saxon's taste reigned supreme. There was a fire here also. Bowls of roses were scattered about; a stack of French novels lay on a bookstand near one of the couches, on which was stretched the skin of a leopard. The effigy of an Indian god held a jewelled casket, which was open, and filled with the most exquisite sweetmeats.

Lady Saxon was not in the room. The servant told Falcon that she had been informed of his arrival, and would appear presently. He lingered, putting another log on the hearth and drawing down the outer blind.

'You prefer this country to Germany?' asked Falcon.

'Ach, yes! Bad-Schwalben is a dreary place in the winter, when the roads are blocked with snow and there is not a single visitor.'

' I should have thought that this place must be quite as dreary as Bad-Schwalben in the winter,' said Falcon.

The man gave his shoulders a shrug, and answered civilly :

'One does not wish for more than the good of his family. Her gracious ladyship has given my wife and son and daughter-in-law a home here.'

'Ah !' said Falcon.

The man withdrew, and in a few minutes Lady Saxon entered. She greeted Falcon

with a certain impetuosity of gesture which
called up the idea that she had thrown off her
shackles, and bade him be seated. She looked
anxious, a little excited, he thought, but quite
at her ease.

'You have cut short your visits in the
country?' he remarked.

'Oh!' She threw up her hands with an
impatient movement. 'Heaven preserve me
from male dummies and fools in petticoats.
Have you heard, my brave Falcon, of that
irresistible longing sometimes which comes
over the civilized savage, to throw off his
clothes and execute a war-dance in his native
paint and feathers? I came here to dance
my war-dance. You may be sure that there
is nobody to tell tales.'

'You are alone, then?'

'Alone!' she repeated sharply. 'Did you
suppose that I had brought Lord Saxon with
me?'

'No, I did not suppose that.'

'Lord Saxon is with the Duke, who has a
fit of the gout. Lord Saxon is one of those
amiable husbands who indulge their wives'
whims, even when the whims are a little

wounding to marital vanity. Lord Saxon is a model of all that is agreeable—in a husband.' She put out her hand and took one of the sweetmeats from the casket, and ate it delicately. 'Will you have one ? They are filled with a liqueur that is as expensive as attar of roses.'

Falcon politely declined the proffered luxury.

'Perhaps you are surprised that I should have sent for you in this sudden sort of way ?' Lady Saxon said, in an abrupt manner.

'No, I am not surprised,' Falcon answered grimly.

'Meaning, I suppose, that nothing I could do would surprise you in the least ?' Lady Saxon said, with a laugh. 'Well, we are confederates—pals, I presume, we may be called, in a sort of way—at least, for one particular purpose——'

'Yes,' Falcon said, with a face of unabated gloom.

'You don't seem as if you altogether liked it ?'

'I am not good at paying compliments, Lady Saxon.'

'I don't want compliments—you may believe I have had my share of them already. Well, I sent for you because I was impatient to know what was going on at Stonehenge Park. Who are there, and what are they doing? I came down here to be near at hand, if there was anything that had to be done.'

'What could there be to be done?' Falcon asked.

'That is exactly what I want to know. Where there are plots there can be counter-plots.'

'I don't know that anything that could be called a plot is going on at Stonehenge Park. There are talks, and perhaps arrangements, about the property claims——'

'Stuff! I don't care about that. I wouldn't have come in this secret way down to this place to hear about some trumpery money claims. Tell me of what I want to know——'

'But, Lady Saxon, I don't understand what you mean—I am too dull to guess. What is it that you want me to tell of?'

'Tell me about the plans for marrying off your Princess—that is what interests me; tell me about *them*——'

'There are no such plans!' Falcon exclaimed angrily, and with a face literally darkened by emotion. 'Who has dared to say that there are any plans like that?'

'You are too simple for this world, General Falcon. I tell you that there are such plans; I will tell you what it seems you don't know, although it is all going on under your very eyes. The priests want your Princess to marry Lord Stonehenge; she herself wants to marry young Bellarmin——'

'Oh!' he exclaimed, and he clenched his hand.

'Yes; in her heart she would like to marry him. She is only a woman, your Princess. And he is handsome and young and fascinating! Oh yes; I can read a woman's heart as well as the heart of a man.'

'Lady Saxon—he! A man of low birth —of no position——'

'Oh! Are you then a prince in disguise, General Falcon? It is not only men of royal lineage who may presume to love your Mary Stuart! But you need not be unhappy about Bellarmin. If it ever comes to a serious ques-

tion with her, and if she has any pride, I
shall be able to settle that matter.'

' You, Lady Saxon! How ?'

' Never mind. All in good time. But
now—now—there is another—now, I am certain—my heart tells me—Victor Champion
wants to marry her! He does! He is there,
is he not—Victor Champion ?—he is there
already ?'

' Yes, he is there; but I believe he has
only come to patter politics with these other
men—he could not have the audacity to
hope——'

' The audacity to hope—and he the greatest
Englishman of his time! The audacity· to
hope what General Falcon hopes! Yes, my
poor Falcon—as your Princess sometimes
calls you—yes; the great man intends to
marry your Princess, if he can.'

' He shall not, by God!' Falcon exclaimed.

' I am glad I have stirred you up at last,
General Falcon—I thought I should find you
sensitive. But how, may I ask, do you intend
to prevent it ? If she doesn't marry Champion she will marry Stonehenge or Bellarmin.
It will be all the same for you.'

'I will do anything to prevent it!' he exclaimed, and he let his hand fall heavily on the table.

'Well, you will have, perhaps, soon to exert all your powers, whatever they are, in that way. Now I will speak out to you—I will act on the square, as they say. I don't mean to let her marry Bellarmin; I don't want her to marry Champion—I couldn't endure *that*; I would rather kill her or myself than have that happen! But, for the rest, I don't care whom she marries, or when she marries, or what happens to her in this world or the next——'

'I wish you wouldn't speak of her in that manner,' Falcon said sternly; 'it is not right for me to hear it.'

A sense of the degradation of his alliance with Lady Saxon was aroused in him as he heard the woman thus speak of his Princess. Lady Saxon understood him, and changed her tone.

'I am sorry if I have hurt you in any way,' she said gently; 'although *she* can laugh at you when she is in the mood for laughter—which I fancy is pretty often.'

'Let us leave her out of our talk as much as we can.'

'Yes, yes; forgive me; but, as you see, I have my own feelings, too, and sometimes they are too strong for me. Well, I want you to be on guard; to keep your eyes and ears open, to see who walks with her most and talks to her most——'

'I can't play the spy, Lady Saxon. That is not at all in my line,' Falcon interposed with a certain dignity.

'Play the spy!' she said contemptuously. 'He calls it playing the spy just to observe what lover comes nearest to the woman he himself loves!'

'Oh, how you degrade her and me!' Falcon groaned.

'Have you no influence over her? Can't you get her away from Stonehenge Park—get her out of Champion's way? I wish we had her here,' she went on in a lighter tone—and all the while she kept her eyes fixed on Falcon's face. 'What a charming bower this would be for a captive Stuart Princess! How safely she might be immured here—kept in gentle and honourable captivity by some gallant Bothwell who wished to save her from political plotters, and prevail on her to marry him! What a charming and romantic notion! She is a romantic young Princess, too. I fancy the enterprise itself would have a charm for her. See, General Falcon,' she rose from her chair and went to the window, drawing aside the curtains that veiled it. 'See how lonely it is in this bay! Look at the descent of that cliff on which our eyry is perched! Look how far down the sea breaks at its feet! Who could come near her without her faithful gaoler's consent? And see my little schooner yacht below—how temptingly it spreads its wings; how easily a yachting excursion might be planned, and the yacht come to an anchor here! One would not need here a company of armed Border men to enact the Bothwell episode.'

General Falcon followed her to the window. He, too, looked out upon the blue, hazy sea, and down at the tarn-like bay, the lonely cliffs to left and right. He turned abruptly away, and paced moodily up and down the room; then he stopped in front of her.

'Lady Saxon,' he said, 'have you any purpose in these strange words?'

'Yes,' she answered boldly. 'I have a purpose, but the time is not ripe for it yet; nor are you, my good Falcon, ripe for it either.'

They were both silent. Falcon's face worked with emotion. A vision of an earthly Paradise opened itself before him. His Mary—his Queen—a captive in his power—alone with him in this wild place, to be won by his daring, by his passionate entreaties, by his deep respect, by his ardent love . . . the bare thought was intoxicating. Lady Saxon watched his face. A kind of reflex emotion kindled in hers. If she herself might only be borne away hither by the man that she loved! Then—let the world go by!

'I wanted you to see this place,' she said presently. 'That is one reason why I sent for you here. If you come to think of any way in which it might be of use to you in your plans, I shall be happy to lend it to you for a week or two. The servants are to be trusted.'

Falcon made no answer. He appeared to

be considering deeply. Lady Saxon left the
window and seated herself on the couch,
which was covered with the leopard-skin.
' Come here,' she said; ' I want to talk to you.
I want to hear about Champion.   How long
has he been at Stonehenge ?'

' Something less than a week.'

' And Bellarmin ?'

' A little longer.'

' A week !' she repeated.   ' And he never
told me that he was going.   Does he talk
with her—hang about her—behave like a
lover ? You know what I mean.   I am speaking of Champion.'

' It appears so.'

' But he is interested in everything that is
new, fresh, picturesque.   Her birth, her position, the historical associations—all this would
attract him.   He has such an extraordinary
power of projecting his sympathies.   It is his
temperament.   I know him so well.'

' You know him so well !' repeated Falcon
slowly.

' It does not mean love,' Lady Saxon went
on, as if speaking to herself, and taking no
notice of Falcon's interruption.   ' He is not

a man to lose his heart to a girl; he who——' Her mind framed the words, 'he who loved *me*.' But she said aloud, 'He who, since he became a widower, might have married any woman in England had he chosen. But the name is historic; he might fancy that such a marriage would increase his power. It would be a mistake. He could not gain anything from her. But it is possible that his imagination might mislead him. His first marriage was a sacrifice to ambition.'

Falcon heard her in grim silence. Then both were silent for a few moments. The minds of both were travelling swiftly through the region of possibilities. Lady Saxon heaved a sigh rather of satisfaction than alarm. She was not afraid. Champion was once more under her influence. This time she could defy ambition.

'When does he leave Stonehenge Park?' she asked, turning on Falcon almost fiercely.

'To-morrow, I understand. The House has already met.' Falcon's tone seemed to indicate resentment at Sir Victor's absence from his Parliamentary post.

'Mere routine business,' said Lady Saxon impatiently. 'And Bellarmin?'

'He, too, goes to-morrow; but they do not travel together. Sir Victor takes an early train.'

'What about Bellarmin and Champion?' Lady Saxon questioned. 'Have they come to any agreement—any political agreement? You know the rumours.'

'I neither know nor care anything about your Parliamentary intrigues, except in so far as they concern the Stuart claims.'

'But you can observe. You know, at least, whether these two have had any private conversation?'

'They walked together for some time on the terrace one morning. I should say they had been talking politics, and that Bellarmin is favourably disposed towards Champion's views, whatever they may be.'

'Ah!' Lady Saxon seemed to be considering deeply. Presently she abruptly changed the conversation. 'I don't wish this visit of yours here talked about.'

Falcon bowed. 'Certainly not, Lady Saxon.'

'There's no object in chatter. Not that I want to make a mystery ; but it would annoy me to be invaded.'

Falcon bowed again.

'I shall return to London in a day or two,' she resumed. 'We shall meet there.'

'You have not forgotten that Wednesday is the date fixed for your dinner-party to Miss Beaton ?'

'No ; I had not forgotten.'

Lady Saxon seemed moody and thoughtful. After a little while General Falcon took his leave, refusing the luncheon which she offered him. He was driven back in the direction whence he had come.

Lady Saxon had a wild impulse to waylay Champion, to bid him come to her at Petrel's Rest. Her heart throbbed at the thought. There had been tender passages between them in London. He had come to the confessional. But her love made her timid. She did not dare to assert her hold upon him too imperiously. There was an iron hand, she knew, beneath the velvet glove. The heart that beat under that caressing manner could be steel at times. She would wind her meshes

more closely round him. She would make
herself necessary to him. She would not re-
sent even his attentions to Mary Beaton.
Her woman's craft got the better of her
woman's impulse. He should not dream that
she suspected him—that she had played the
spy. She told herself that she understood
the reason why he had dallied at Stonehenge
Park. He did not wish to appear too eager.
It would not be wise to let Bellarmin imagine
that the trap had been laid and baited, and
that he was to be secured forthwith. She
told herself all this. Nevertheless, she wrote
to Champion a letter, which should meet him
in London—a letter, in its earlier pages, more
political than personal, ignoring the fact that
he had not told her of his proposed visit
to Lord Stonehenge, but taking for granted
that he had accepted the invitation in order
to gain a good opportunity of getting at
Bellarmin's views. Bellarmin's adhesion ob-
tained, and with it the chance of his band
being augmented by other Democratic Tories,
and also the adhesion of the extreme Radical
or Tressel Party ; then the Whig section, in
the person of her husband, might be cautiously

attacked. Lady Saxon gauged the situation with a keenness and grasp that might have been envied by many a trained politician. She threw out subtle suggestions, showing a man's courage and a woman's finesse. She gave adroit hints concerning the wires by which certain of the political puppets might be pulled to his side. He should see clearly that her influence was far-reaching, that her assistance was not to be despised.

And then from a politician she became suddenly a woman of the world—bright, amusing, witty. She described her country-house visits with a satirical humour—a clever seizing of characteristic points only possible to one who had regarded life from another level. It was a very well-schemed letter. There was a touch of veiled sentiment at the end, a note of repressed passion, a suggestion of regret amid all the splendours which surrounded her—regret half bitter, half melancholy, for the 'beautiful past'—that, had Champion failed to be touched by it, would have proved him something more than man.

Champion's answer arrived by return of post. It was couched in the brilliant, tender, poetic style, peculiarly his own, and which, when he chose to employ it in winning a woman, became irresistible. Lady Saxon did not object to a certain delicate diplomatic reserve. She was alive to the desirability of caution in the correspondence of a statesman. At least, he showed her that he understood her talent and her power, and he appreciated and frankly accepted her devotion to his interests.

CHAPTER VII.

LORD SAXON.

LORD SAXON sat in his study one morning. His face wore a troubled look. He had been reading the papers, and the papers had a bad effect on him. The papers were most of them full of attacks upon Champion. This in itself would have annoyed Saxon, but there were other considerations too. He saw that nearly all the papers had got filled with the idea that Champion was planning some grand *coup* to make himself more popular than ever, and to get himself back into office; and he did not believe in anything of the kind; it was all lies and nonsense. Still, the lies and nonsense vexed and disturbed Lord Saxon all the same.

If you feel perfectly well, and people come
telling you one after the other that you look
very unwell, you may not believe them, but
their assurances make you feel uncomfortable.
So with Lord Saxon. He did not believe
that his friend and leader was deceiving him ;
but to be always reading assertions which
pointed that way made him feel not exactly
distrustful, but decidedly uncomfortable.

Lady Saxon had, he knew, gone off on one
of her eccentric trips to Petrel's Rest. He
was expecting her return some time during
the day, for he had been given to understand
that they had a dinner-party that evening.
Suddenly she burst in upon him in all the
glory of her beauty and her splendid vitality,
and with a certain radiance of the morning
about her.

'Well, Josephine,' Lord Saxon said in his
ineffusive manner ; but a change came over his
face as she entered, and the cloud lightened.

'You didn't expect me quite so early, dear.
I wasn't altogether sure myself that I could
get up in time for the first train. But it was
lovely driving over the moors this morning ;
and I had things I wanted to see about. I

am too late for your breakfast though, I see.
No, I don't want anything more. I had
some coffee at a station. Have you been dull
these days, breakfasting without me ?'

It was Lady Saxon's chief concession to
the domestic virtues to breakfast late every
morning with her husband. It kept him in
a good humour—not that Lord Saxon was
ever in a bad humour with her. It made him
believe in her; and she got over her duty
early in the day, 'swallowed her physic before
it had time to stand,' as she put it to herself.

' Yes, of course—you know,' he said with
awkward fondness.

He did not ask what she had been doing
at Petrel's Rest. She had long ago given
him to understand that she did not choose to
be asked questions about her movements, and
that he must be content with such information as she herself volunteered. Lord Saxon
was not inquisitive, and made much concession to his wife's mood. On the whole, the
strain of independence and originality in her
pleased him. And then he was always delighted to have her with him, ready to take
her on her own terms.

Yet in spite of her radiance and her beauty she seemed agitated, excited, he thought. Something had put her out. 'Women are easily put out,' Lord Saxon reflected. It is their way; if not, they wouldn't be women—certainly not charming women.

'You were looking worried,' Lady Saxon said. 'What is the matter? Anything wrong in politics?'

'Nothing that I know of. I have been reading the papers, and I'm so sorry poor old Greenleaf—don't you know—is dead.' He read her a paragraph from a paper:

'Death of a veteran M.P.—We regret to announce the sudden death of Mr. Greenleaf, one of the oldest members of the House of Commons, and who represented the same constituency for more than fifty years. The death was sudden; it took place in the House of Commons library about two o'clock yesterday. Mr. Greenleaf was reading in the library, and perhaps had fallen asleep. Some of the officials of the House were testing the division bells; and the bells were made to ring sharply. Mr. Greenleaf started up on hearing the sound, and was heard to cry, "A division already?" and he ran towards the door. The only other member in the library was Mr. Bellarmin; and Mr. Bellarmin called out, "No, no; they are only trying the bells; the House is not sitting." Mr. Greenleaf, however, hurried on, and just as he reached the nearest door he fell on the floor. Mr. Bellarmin and one of the librarians ran to his assistance, but they found that the poor old gentleman was dead. It used to be a boast of Mr. Greenleaf's that he never missed a division of the House.'

'Poor old creature!' Lady Saxon said carelessly. 'It was the right sort of way for him to die.'

'Seems to me terrible,' Lord Saxon said; 'a sudden death like that. Fancy being full of life one minute and dead the next!'

'Oh! but a poor old thing like that—what did it matter?'

'Sudden death is not only for the old. Poor Greenleaf!'

'Why, Saxon, you are quite tragic over this dreadful old man. He had lived long enough.'

Lord Saxon said no more on that subject.

His wife evidently could not be got to feel for poor old Greenleaf and his sudden death. Lord Saxon turned listlessly to some other part of the paper he held in his hand. Lord Saxon felt that one of the duties of his position was to read the papers every morning, and accordingly he read them. Sometimes they made him very angry ; more often they made him yawn. 'The fellows seem to know so little about anything,' Lord Saxon often said. He was very conscious of his own defective education ; and he was satisfied, in a stolid, resigned sort of way, that his was a very slow intelligence. When he found that on some political question he knew more of the realities of things than some writer of a leading article in a newspaper, he was not elated, he was merely disappointed. This day he was particularly displeased.

'What's the good of reading a paper if the fellows who write don't know half as much as one knows one's self ?' he said irrelevantly, without waiting for an answer to his question, as he tossed aside one of the dailies over which he had been poring.

Lord Saxon was a man absolutely without

self-conceit. He honestly understood his own capacity, and was inclined to overrate the abilities of others. He was selfish in a certain sense—that is to say, he did not know how to deny himself any momentary gratification which he coveted; but in a broader sense he often showed himself quietly self-sacrificing. He stuck to politics and the House of Commons because the family traditions and his father's wish told him that he ought to do so; and he had even drilled himself into an interest in politics, and had trained and hammered himself into a really powerful, hard-hitting, straight-from-the-shoulder sort of Parliamentary debater. He was often taken for a haughty and sullen man, when he was, in fact, only shy, slow of speech, and awkward. A spoilt child, he had at least some of the characteristic virtues of spoilt childhood if he had most of its characteristic vices. He loved his father dearly, and thus far he adored his wife: he put absolute trust in her.

Lady Saxon stepped rapidly towards her husband, and stood for a moment behind his chair, looking at him with a curious contemptuous smile on her face before she spoke.

'What is the good of reading the papers?' she said. 'Well, I like to make sure that "the fellows" don't know what I know. Think of the thousands of people who read those articles as if they were gospel. It amuses me to know that I am ever so much better informed than they are. It's like having private proof of the spuriousness of the Bible, or like hearing a man tell the House of Commons from the Treasury Bench that the Government never did make certain proposals to some foreign Power after he has himself shown you in confidence a copy of the despatch and the reply. Well, but what have the papers been saying now?'

'Stuff about Champion.'

'But they are always talking stuff about Champion. What are they saying now?'

'Saying that he is planning some great *coup*—some popular thing—to get back into office.'

'I wish to Heaven he were!' Lady Saxon said emphatically.

Lord Saxon looked up amazed.

'Why so, Josephine?'

'Because I am ambitious for him and for you. I hate to see two such men out of office. You ought to be in power; you ought to be governing England—you two. Why, your father says it himself—he said it to me the other day.'

'Ah, but he might not quite like some of Champion's notions, all the same.'

'He would when he came to understand them,' Lady Saxon said, in a tone of decision.

Lord Saxon was a little puzzled by his wife's manner.

'Did you see Champion when you were at Petrel's Rest?' he asked suddenly.

'Why should I? I went away for quiet. No; I didn't go near Stonehenge Park. I didn't want to go there. I didn't fancy myself with all these Jacobites and Legitimists. But Sir Victor Champion, of course, thinks it is his business to know everybody— and he is quite right.'

'Of course; of course.' Lord Saxon was turning over something slowly in the recesses of his mind. At last he seemed anxious to put away the topic of conversation.

'By the way, Josephine, who are coming to dinner to-day ?—besides Champion, I mean.'

Lady Saxon had moved from him and begun to open some letters which she had brought in with her.

'Who are coming to dinner to-day ?' she said presently. 'The Princess, of course, to begin with.'

'The Princess ? Which Princess ?'

'The Stuart Princess; the young Pretendress; the lovely Jacobite.'

'Miss Beaton, do you mean ?'

'Miss Beaton, yes.'

'Dear Josephine,' Lord Saxon said, with a heavy smile, 'don't call her a Princess, please. She isn't any Princess. I wonder if she has any sense that she can let people talk about her in that way—it's nonsense.'

'I suppose she likes it. It was only my fun, dear, calling her a Princess. I wish you would pay her some attention, Saxon; it would look well from you. And she is so much admired.'

'Oh! she is a deuced nice-looking girl, and

all that,' Lord Saxon conceded, not with the air of one who is deeply engrossed in the subject ; 'and Champion thinks her clever— so I am told.'

'Told—by whom ?' Lady Saxon's voice had a little suggestion of sharpness in it as she put the question to her unconcerned husband.

'Don't quite remember, Josephine, I'm sure. Everybody, I think.'

'The people who are coming!—let me see.' She named two or three great political peers.

'Oh, that lot!' her husband said, with an air of profound depression.

'Must, Saxon, must—you grumbling person. They want to meet the fair Princess—oh! I beg pardon—of course, I mean Miss Mary Beaton.'

'All right, Josephine. Is there no one new or interesting except Miss Beaton ?'

'I don't know whether you would call her aide-de-camp, or master of the horse, or what-ever he is, interesting, General Falcon.'

'Certainly not,' Lord Saxon replied promptly, for him. 'And do you know, Josephine,' he said, partly rousing himself up, 'there's something odd about that man—something I can't quite make out. I must have seen him somewhere—I can't remember if that's it. His face impresses me in a devilish uncomfortable sort of manner—kind of man to cut his throat, or do something of that kind, in some odd, unexpected public way.'

'My dear Saxon, what very horrible ideas! But we have to ask him, you know; and that dreadful old Lady Struthers. They are supposed to be in attendance on Miss Beaton, and they would expect to be asked.'

'Oh, of course—of course; they would expect to be asked.'

'There is Mr. Bellarmin. Do you call him interesting?'

'Yes, I call him interesting. He is coming to the front in the House—I should like to see more of him.'

'You might easily do that; he comes here very often,' Lady Saxon replied carelessly.

'To your luncheons, I suppose. That set isn't in my line.'

'Not political enough,' suggested Lady Saxon; 'though that doesn't quite apply.'

‘No. They are too——I don’t care about their talk—too many fireworks.’

‘Let us say that they are too epigrammatic for you,’ said Lady Saxon. ‘You must have had some of Mr. Bellarmin’s fireworks in the House.’

‘Oh, he is a clever fellow. Some people say he is self-conceited and a puppy and all that; but I don’t quite think it of him. He would get on if he had money, but I am told he has no money; and by Jove, Josephine, it’s hard for a fellow to get on—no matter how clever he may be—without money. I have thought of that sometimes.’

Lady Saxon had thought of it a good deal in former days, and could have illustrated it by experiences of her own had she been so minded. Just now, however, she did not care to pursue the theme.

‘Well, that’s about the whole lot,’ she said, when she had given him the names of a few more of their guests.

Lord Saxon went back abruptly to Bellarmin.

‘Bellarmin’s looking out for a woman with money, I have heard men say. I should think he could find one easily enough—he is a handsome, well-set-up fellow. But that always seemed to me the deuce of being poor—that one has to look out not for the woman he would like to marry, but for the woman with money.'

He looked at his wife as he spoke. Lady Saxon smiled on him with gracious affection.

'Now,' Lord Saxon went on, in a meditative way; 'if a girl like Miss Beaton had money and were to take a real fancy for a young fellow like Bellarmin, that wouldn't be half a bad thing for both of them. They say he sticks very closely to her.'

Lady Saxon winced and chafed under these remarks. She would not so much have minded the idea of Bellarmin's marrying for money; but it made the nerves of her vanity sore to hear him talked of as an admirer of Miss Beaton. And if Saxon of all men had heard of such a thing, and noticed and remembered it, rumour could not speak altogether falsely.

'My dear Saxon, it is something new to hear you entering into these marriage speculations and love-makings! I never thought you observed things of that kind.'

'One sometimes observes more than people fancy, Josephine.'

The words were carelessly spoken, and had no special meaning. Lord Saxon was feeling a little surprised at himself for indulging in so much gossip, and was wondering where he had got it. But Lady Saxon almost started; and she turned her head away for a moment.

'You were speaking of Sir Victor Champion,' she said presently, in her tenderest tone; 'I want you to think about him, Saxon.'

'My dear Josephine, I think a lot about him; I am always thinking about him, more or less.'

'But I want you to believe in him; to trust him; to trust in him; to trust in him fully; to have entire faith in him; to trust yourself to him. He is a great man; all his views are great. I want you and him to govern England together.'

She came over to him and leaned upon his shoulder, and bent her head down winningly over his and gazed into his eyes. He did not understand her; he had no perception of her meaning; but he felt the fascination of her manner and her eyes.

'Look here,' she went on earnestly, and with that dash of the melodramatic which had grown to be characteristic of her; 'I want you to be a great man, Saxon; my husband! I want to be proud of you; I *am* proud of you, as it is; but I want you to do great things; I want you to be a great English statesman. You have all the brains and all the courage——'

'Not all the brains, Josephine, dear; no—no; but I hope I have courage enough—if one only saw one's way, and if——'

Lord Saxon paused, and sighed in a heavy perplexed manner, strange in one ordinarily so stolid and composed. Lady Saxon did not notice the sigh, but exclaimed eagerly:

'Exactly; there it is. One don't always see one's own way; and then is the time for trusting someone who does.'

Lord Saxon raised his head a little, and looked at her in some surprise.

'Yes, Saxon; I know what I am saying. Sometimes, perhaps, you may not quite see your way—you are a slow old darling now and then ; but when you do see your way, who can tread it so firmly and so boldly as you can ? Oh, I have been so proud of you often—proud of my husband. Dear, I couldn't care for any man in all the world if he were not ambitious—ambitious of greatness.'

'But, Josephine, my dear—I don't understand ; really I don't.'

'It's this ; Victor Champion always sees his way. No man in England can read the signs of the times as he can. I want you to go with him ; to believe and to know that what he does is wise and right ; and not to let anyone estrange you from him. You must promise me that! You will promise me that ?'

She threw her arms fondly round his neck, and drew his head closer to her.

Saxon faintly struggled with the embrace ; but only in order to give expression to his perplexities.

'Well, but, Josephine, who talks about our being estranged ? Are we not the best of friends ? Why, everyone knows that I am devoted to him. They are always reproaching me with being too devoted to him—some of them are.   What does it all mean ?   Is he really planning something ?'

'Dear, how should I know ?   But of course his mind is always full of England's future ; of course he must be thinking of something great.   Whatever it is, I want *you* to be in it.   Promise me, Saxon, that you will not lightly allow any people or any idle talk to come between you and him.   You must promise me *that ;* I ask it for your own sake. I want to see you and him always associated —I want you and him to govern England.'

'Josephine,' Lord Saxon said gravely, 'there are only three people in the world, I think, that I care for really—and you know who they are—yourself, and my old Governor, and Champion.   It would be a curious thing that you and Champion wanted me to do and that I did not do, wouldn't it ?   You wouldn't ask me to do anything that I oughtn't to do ; and neither would he, I am sure.   So there's nothing to promise, is there ?'

'That is promise enough,' she said, and she touched his forehead with her lips.

He drew her down to him closer, and folded one arm about her, gazing up at her beautiful face, which she held back slightly averted. Something of almost poetic yearning shone in Lord Saxon's dull eyes, and lightened his heavy, reddened features. For a moment or two he did not speak.

'Well?' she asked laughingly. 'Bear! What is it? You have been so remarkably sociable of late, that I have almost forgotten my nickname for you.'

'Have I been less bearish in society of late, Josephine? I am never bearish to *you*.'

'Never, dear—I must pay you that compliment. But, really, your sublime resignation to circumstances while we were doing our visits was something beautiful to behold. It was I who showed the wild beast, and had to run off to my lair.'

'I wonder why you like to rush off in that wild way to Petrel's Rest; and why you won't let me go with you. I should enjoy doing " Darby and Joan " there with you once or twice in the season, Josephine. I get a little tired of it all.'

' " Darby and Joan," and " John Anderson my Jo," are not in my line, Saxon, as I told you when we married, dear. Nevertheless, if you wish it, I am willing to do that or anything else, at one of the other places—not at Petrel's Rest.   That's my own particular lair ; and I love it the more because *you* gave it to me to growl in, and because you are such a gentleman, Saxon, that you respect my whim still. A woman likes that, you know——'

'You are a strange creature, Josephine,' he said in fond pride.

'You knew that from the first.   I always told you that I wasn't the Patient Grizel sort of woman, or the conventional beggar-maid, who waited so submissively for King Cophetua to step down to her.   I have often thought that the beggar-maid must have felt the pinch of her gold-embroidered shoes, and must have longed to take them off and go barefoot again now and then.   I have walked barefoot, Saxon —yes, barefoot after a caravan, when I was a little girl ; and I too have felt the craving to take off my smart shoes sometimes.   But Queen Cophetua wouldn't have liked her king to see her when she had one of her wild fits on.   She would have wanted to go all alone from the Palace, and forget for a little while that she was a Queen.'

' But she would have been glad to come back to the Palace and to Cophetua once more ; and she might not be sorry then that she was a Queen,' said Saxon tenderly.

' Dear Bear — dear practical, statistical politician ! can it be possible that *I* am making you poetic ?'

' I don't pretend to be poetic, or out of the common, or—or anything like you, Josephine.' Lord Saxon reddened to a deeper tint than even was natural to him. ' But I think I'm not quite the stolid, statistical sort of person you make me out, or I couldn't have wanted so madly to marry you. There never was a woman in the world that suited me as you do—and I couldn't have cared for you if you had been the conventional kind—of one sort or the other. I've known plenty of them— Grizels and Vere de Veres, and beggar- maids, too, by Jove !—and you were the only one I wanted to settle down with as my wife. Perhaps I'm slow at showing what I feel. You don't like me to be demonstrative ; you don't like to be effusive either, and I'm not sure if I don't admire you all the more for that— but there it is. It's a fact. And sometimes, by Jove, Josephine! I wish that we could leave it all—the show and the business and the House of Commons—for a bit, and go and set up a cabin somewhere in the Wild West by ourselves.'

'That wouldn't please me, Saxon, for more than a day or two. The show and the business is what I like, just as I liked the booths and the fairs in the old caravan days. You know I never pretended to you that I was anything but a caravan child, who might have grown up to be something too dreadful to think about, if a kind, generous man hadn't been touched by my youth and my innocence'—Lady Saxon gave a queer little half-pathetic laugh as she spoke—'and my beauty, I suppose, and if he hadn't taken me away and educated me and married me. The taint of the caravan clings to me still. I like glitter and show. I like a retinue, I like— this——' and she waved her hand towards the splendidly furnished room. 'But you— well, I can understand that the society business bores you. You should be glad that you have a wife who is capable of doing it alone, and will leave you with your blue-

books in peace. . . . But the real business
of your life—you couldn't get away from it if
you would, and you would not if you could
—politics, statesmanship, government! All
that. It's in your blood. You have inherited it from the Athelstanes and the
Saxons and the rest. Do not think I am not
proud of that! *This* is your part in the world,
and I want to spur you on to reform of old
abuses, to power, to the governing of a great
nation. It is to this you will come if you join
Victor Champion.'

She had moved from him as she talked, and
stood before him, her eyes alight, her bosom
heaving.

A vague expression of doubt and trouble
crept over Saxon's face.

'Can there be anything? Are the papers
on the scent? . . . Do you know anything,
Josephine? It is not possible. I will not
believe that Champion could have spoken of
any project he may have in his mind to *anyone* before he spoke to me.'

'No, no!' exclaimed Lady Saxon eagerly,
'how could you imagine it? But I have
intuitions—even you have said so. Didn't I

foretell Glengordon's resignation ?   I can read
the signs of the times more quickly than you.
There will be a change—a great scheme—
and Champion will speak of it first to you—
to whom else ?'

Saxon rose from his seat with a reluctant,
preoccupied air.   'Well, it will come, if it is
to come,' he said slowly.   'Not too soon, I
hope.'

' I hope that it will come before the Session
is over,' she answered ; 'and that England
will have to thank you for a big thing.'

' You are all at me,' Saxon went on—' you,
the Governor, the papers, everyone.   You
all talk of my doing something big before—
before——'   He hesitated.

' Before you fossilize in the House of Lords
as Duke of Athelstane,' she put in.

' No—yes.   I sometimes think, Josephine,
that you will never be Duchess of Athelstane.'

' What do you mean ?' she asked, her face
blanching.   This was a contingency she
had never contemplated.   She *meant* to be
Duchess of Athelstane.   'You are not ill,
Saxon—you—why, you look in the most
robust health.'

'I am big enough, and red enough, and muscular enough, and all that,' he answered, laughing a little grimly. 'But I didn't want to frighten you, Josephine. I did not really mean that the Governor might outlive me, though I shouldn't be surprised at it. He is better after the grouse on the moors than I am. I don't quite know why I said that, unless it's because I have been feeling rather down lately—a fit of the blue-devils—a sort of lethargy, and queer sensations now and then. Liver, I suppose. Everything is liver with us London men. We smoke too much, and drink too much, and live too hard when we are young fellows.'

'You should see a doctor,' said Lady Saxon. 'I have often told you, dear, that it is a sluggish liver that makes you so disinclined to go out among people. Call in Geddes; I wonder why you have such an invincible objection to being photographed and to seeing a doctor?'

'Perhaps because I am afraid of the result in both cases,' answered Lord Saxon. 'I know that I'm not a beauty, and I've always had a queer instinctive kind of notion that I was not altogether sound in the wind. Anyhow, I hope that I am not a coward, and if there should be anything wrong with me, I'd rather know it. I'd rather know *anything* than live on in a fool's paradise. A fellow can take a long breath then, and look round him. There's only one thing—by Jove, Josephine, if you were to play me false, I'd rather be hoodwinked into believing you true !'

Lady Saxon kept her eyes lowered. 'You love me so much, then ! I am glad. About this doctor ? I am anxious.'

'Oh, I am rather ashamed of having got funked. I was so blue last night that I wrote a note to Scourfield making an appointment. I shall look in on him on my way to the House.'

'Scourfield !' repeated Lady Saxon, for her husband had named a famous specialist. She made no further comment, however, and they separated.

Lady Saxon thought no more of her husband. She went to plan the arrangement of her little dinner-party. She liked to plan her dinner-parties. Lord Saxon's house had become famous for its little dinners since Lady Saxon had become its mistress. Lord Saxon's father made it his study to advance his son to political leadership. It was a fine tradition in that great Whig family that the eldest son should always be a political leader in the House of Commons, and that the father should find liberal means for the elder son to fulfil all the social as well as the political duties of leadership. The Duke of Athelstane had wished his eldest son to be married as soon as possible, and to be married to the daughter of some great English Whig peer. But Lord Saxon disappointed his father in the two conditions : he did not marry early, and he did not marry the daughter of an English Whig peer. He remained until his fortieth year unmarried, and then he came home from Germany bringing with him as his wife the widow of a doubtful baron, some Residenz doctor who had been ennobled because he restored to imaginary health a dyspeptic or hypochondriacal German prince. Still, the Duke was heroic enough to make the best of things even then. Lord Saxon's reckless youth had inspired the Duke with a secret dread that he might be entrapped by even a less eligible co-mate than this widow of a doubtful German baron. And there were other and more occult reasons, which, however, the Duke would not readily have acknowledged, that made him willing to indulge his son in all ways.

So Lord Saxon's father accepted Lady Saxon, and even put on a goodly show of welcome for her. She was very handsome; she proved to be very clever, and there was nothing against her—at least, there was nothing known against her; and she flattered the old man a great deal, and before long had talked him over. Lady Saxon's father-in-law came to put some trust in her, and to regard her as a sort of fellow-conspirator and colleague. She had a genius for political combinations and for dinner-parties, and the head of the house gave her full means of testing her capacity. The Duke was old, and was anxious that his son should make a name and an influence in the House of Commons before destiny, cruel in two ways, should remove the father from the House of Lords and entomb the son alive in the father's vacated place. Thus the stiff festivities at the family mansion, in which men only had taken part, now gave place to a more brilliant and even more lavish form of entertainment at the house in Seamore Place.

CHAPTER VIII.

LADY SAXON'S DINNER-PARTY.

LORD AND LADY SAXON were in their drawing-room receiving their guests. Lady Saxon, full of animation and talk, looked more than usually Juno-like and magnificent in her rich draperies and her wonderful parure of uncut sapphires and diamonds. Who could have believed, even on her own confession, that she had once walked barefooted behind a caravan? Lord Saxon, on the other hand, was duller and heavier than his wont. He had a stupid, preoccupied air, and when he spoke he seemed hardly to lift his eyes from the ground.

Lord Saxon's father, the Duke of Athelstane, had arrived. He was a hale, handsome, erect old man, who, people said, looked, but for his white hair, younger, straighter, and of keener vitality than his son. There had also come the Duke of Nornside, old-young, dandified, unmarried—to the eternal disgrace of chaperones—who had succeeded to his dukedom in his minority, and who prided himself upon having seen a good deal more of the world than most people—all other Dukes included ; his mother, the Duchess of Nornside ; an Archbishop, and several people belonging entirely to the world of fashion and politics.

Presently Mr. Bellarmin was announced. Despite all his recent troubles of spirit, he seemed to bring with him that which was his peculiar charm—a certain breath of youth and sweetness and enjoyment of life, not altogether congenial with that somewhat luxurious and languorous atmosphere.

'Anything in your House to-day, Mr. Bellarmin ?' the Duke of Nornside asked.

'No, nothing to speak of—a local Sunday Closing Bill ; it was talked out. By the way, you weren't there, Lord Saxon ?'

'No,' returned Lord Saxon monosyllabically; and Lady Saxon darted a glance at her husband. For the first time since the morning it occurred to her that he had seen Sir Oscar Scourfield that day.

The Duke of Nornside began to talk politics at once. It was not that he took great interest in the subject ; but he had a way of talking familiarly about anything that came up, whether he knew much about it or not. 'I dare say you fellows are breaking your hearts to get back into office, eh, Saxon ? eh, Mr. Bellarmin ? Are you and your Tory Democrats—your merry men—isn't that what Tommy Tressel calls them ?—going to help these Liberal fellows to get back again ?'

Bellarmin smiled, and made a jesting rejoinder. Lord Saxon's heavy brows met in a slight frown. The Duke of Nornside never allowed himself to be disturbed by the consciousness of having made a *malapropos* remark, and added a few more in the same strain.

' The system of government by party is really deplorable,' said the Archbishop, shaking his head despondingly.

'But what to put in its place?   That's the point,' cheerfully observed the elder Duke.

'We don't want to get into office,' broke in Lord Saxon brusquely.   'Fact of it is, what the country wants now is quiet.   We have been putting in a lot of change lately; and I am sure people want to be let alone now for a little.   So do I.'

'Yes, but people say that Lucifer is getting restless.   He wants to stir up the Constitution, don't he?—to make a sensation?' said the Duke of Nornside.

'I don't believe a word of what people or the men on the papers say; it's they who want to stir up things for a sensation,' said Lord Saxon decisively.   'Champion's all right.'

'You are a great believer in Champion, Lord Saxon,' the Archbishop said, with another shake of his head.

'Well, naturally.   I *am* a great believer in Champion.   He gets hold of the people somehow—don't you know?   One can't tell how he does it.   Wonderful head!'

'Wonderful voice!' the Archbishop conceded.

' Wonderful tongue!' the Duke of Nornside put in.

' Yes, he has a wonderful tongue,' Lord Saxon replied simply. ' But it is not all tongue, as some of you fellows try to make out. You say that you believe it ; but I don't fancy you really do. Champion is a great man ; and of course he is a great friend of mine.'

' But you don't want to go in for all sorts of revolutionary schemes — abolishing the House of Lords and all that ?'

' Of course I don't ; but no one does. Don't you believe a word of it.'

' Still, by Jove !' the Duke exclaimed, ' you know everybody is saying things, and everybody can't be wrong.'

' Everybody ? Who is everybody ? The fellows on the evening papers ? or Tommy Tressel ?'

' No ; Tommy Tressel told me it was bosh, and that there was nothing going on ; but I always believed all the more that there was something. I know Tommy was only trying to put me off the scent.'

' But you don't really imagine,' Saxon said

very gravely, and supporting his chin with one hand while he looked fixedly at the young Duke, and his face wore an expression not altogether unlike a scowl—' you really don't imagine that Champion would, in any case, make a confidant of Tommy Tressel? Come, you can't believe that?'

' Don't know what I might not believe of Champion.'

Lord Saxon's face changed its frown or scowl into a rugged smile.

' I verily believe,' he said, ' some of you fellows think Champion is the devil.' And just at this moment the name of Sir Victor Champion was announced.

Sir Victor paused for half a second on the threshold, and flashed his deep brown eyes round the room and over the company. His eyes had the peculiarity of seeming to rest on every one in a company at the same moment; and Champion could always individualize with a glance every one of such a group. Lady Saxon went forward to meet him. There was a radiancy about her as she held out her hand. She felt sure that things were going well with him; and she had a sort of pride of ownership in him and his plans just then.   She thought there was something significant in the very pressure of his hand.   He began to talk at once ; ostensibly to the Duchess of Nornside, really to the company generally, about some new play which he had seen and admired ; and he even quoted some lines from it, giving them out with far finer dramatic effect than can always be commanded by actors even of the highest class.   While he was still declaiming, Mary Beaton was announced.   Perhaps no other comer could have drawn attention away just then from Champion's declamation ; but the curiosity about Miss Beaton was intense and overpowering, and Champion stopped in the middle of a sentence.   Even the Archbishop was not so devoted, or so bigoted in his devotion, to the Act of Settlement as not to be curious to see something of the young lady who was given out as a Stuart Princess, and was alleged to have at least a moral right to the Crown of England.

Bellarmin, recaught in the toils of Lady Saxon, with whom he had been exchanging a few low-toned words, half bantering, half serious, about what she called 'the Stonehenge negotiations,' turned, too, at Mary's entrance.

Though it was in reality only a day or two since he had parted from her, there seemed a lapse of years between then and now, and he had a fantastic sense of a gulf fixed between them.   He had returned to London with the determination to put away all hope of winning her, to deck himself once more in Lady Saxon's gilded chains, and to deaden the tender memories of Stonehenge Park by plunging into the whirl of social and political excitement.   But everything seemed to stand still for him as she approached, and the lights and the forms and the faces of the people round him, and even Lady Saxon herself, in all her luxuriant beauty, paled and dimmed and became unreal as the phantoms of the Walpurgis night might have seemed to Faust when he beheld the vision of Margaret.   How fair and sweet and noble she looked—his White Queen—as she paused, with a certain stately expectation, just within the threshold of the door, and seemed to wait for her host to lead her forward.   Mary Stuart Beaton might in truth have been the Blanche Reine, for, true to her traditions, she had arranged her costume of stiff white brocade, with its pointed bodice and straight folds, and a curious little coif of rose diamonds upon her chestnut hair, so as to forcibly suggest her illustrious ancestress of unhappy memory; while General Falcon, with a foreign star and order on his breast, and Lady Struthers, in ruby velvet and Venetian point lace, seemed by no means unfitting attendants to a young lady of royal descent.

Lord and Lady Saxon advanced to welcome her, the latter with considerable effusiveness; and the Duke of Athelstane, the Archbishop and the Duke of Nornside were presented.

Lady Saxon did not approve of what she called the *table-d'hôte* system of dining. She had arranged this dinner after a plan of her own. She broke up the dining-room into several small tables, each accommodating six persons. She carefully arranged who was to dine with whom, and thus made thoughtful provision for each party to allow of political combinations and political confidences, with a leaven of beauty and wit and fashion to give vivacity to the lump.

There were three tables set out this evening. Lord Saxon presided at one, Lady Saxon at another, and the Duke of Athelstane at the third table. If you did not sit with Lord Saxon, then perhaps you sat with Lady Saxon—and you could not grumble at that; and if not with Lady Saxon, then be pleased to remember that you sat with the grandest old Whig peer in England, the living head of the house of which Lord Saxon was only the heir-apparent. There! Thus each guest might reason to himself.

At Lord Saxon's table sat Mary Beaton, Sir Victor Champion—had Lady Saxon displayed her usual generalship in this respect? —but she had so arranged that she could watch him from where she sat, and she had placed the two as far apart as is possible at a round table—the Duke of Nornside, Lady Mavis Redhouse, who was tall and dark and had a fixed dreamy smile, and was, in fact, or liked to be thought, the Primrose League Egeria of the ultra-Tory Party; and Lady Eastgrave, a beauty in her meridian, who wore a marvellous Paris costume of black and yellow, and whom Lady Saxon had placed there with an artistic sense of variety as presenting an exact contrast to the modern Mary Stuart. Lady Eastgrave had yellow hair—not bright gold like Lady Saxon's, but a beautiful *crêpé* arrangement fresh from Bond Street, which only the eye of a hairdresser—or a woman—could detect as *postiche*, yet which seemed worn more as a concession to fashion than with a view to artifice. She had black eyebrows and clear dark eyes, and the thin high-featured face which one associates with a certain type of the English aristocracy—the type which holds its head erect and looks vacuous and bored as it tools along the Ladies' Mile, which clips its *g*'s with high-bred scorn, and languidly vituperates Radical abuses, and is never anything but Whig-Tory or Tory-Whig. Lady Eastgrave's colour was a little fixed, and her diamonds were magnificent. She seemed at once ingenuous and blasée, and turned directly to Miss Beaton and made a remark on some commonplace subject, which, however, conveyed with fine directness, ' I know who you are, and I want you to know that I know.'

Mary Beaton, seated between her heavy

taciturn host and the young Duke of Nornside, had an opportunity for making a mental note upon the lack of brilliancy displayed by the British peer. Lord Saxon said very little, and there were long pauses between his sentences. He asked some questions about the little Schwalbenstadt Court. His notions about the government of Schwalbenstadt appeared dim, and he was constantly recurring to Frankfort—a city which seemed to have made a more abiding impression upon him than any other he had ever visited. This was natural, perhaps; but Mary did not know that it was there he had married Madame Langenwelt, and so was at a loss to understand why German life should be regarded solely from the standpoint of Frankfort-on-the-Maine. Then Lord Saxon said that he thought English people were worse educated in the matter of geography than any other people on the face of the globe; and he told Mary that he was always busy—that he didn't find being out of office made much difference in the amount of work that he got through; and that if a fellow did his duty conscientiously in the House of Commons, and got up his

facts, there was no time for anything else—
the only result of being in office was that
you had to trust to other people to get up
your facts for you ; but he always liked to get
up his own facts if he could.

The Duke, on the other side, kept up a
sort of rippling monologue. He was very
good-looking. The aroma of rank and fashion
which seemed to exhale from him would have
delighted the lady novelists who make their
heroes talk French, and who revel in 'le
high-life.' The Duke did not talk French or
even very grammatical English. He, too,
clipped his '*g*'s,' and he drawled a little, and
put in 'don't you know' at the end of every
sentence. His eyes had a funny twinkle ; he
looked exquisitely clean and well got-up. His
hair was shorn very close and parted in the
middle ; and he seemed to feel that his station
involved certain duties, one of which was that
of being affable to everybody.

The Duke asked, too, about Schwalbenstadt.
He was very communicative about his opinions
and his fancies. He was very fond of travelling. He always had travelled a great deal.
In fact, he would like to be at it now, going

round the world on a bicycle, don't you know,
and that sort of thing. 'But I am tied by
the leg. Must stop in England. Fact is,
I'm a conscientious fellow. In these times I
think a fellow ought to stay at home. It's
his duty, don't you know, and a word to his
people now and then, and seeing to his farms,
and making friends out in the hunting-field,
and that sort of thing ; why, it might help to
stop a revolution, don't you see, and everyone says there is a revolution coming.'

The Duke paused and looked at Mary, not
certain as to how far he was treading on
personal grounds. 'I hope you are not
going to start a revolution, Miss Beaton.
It would lead to no end of bothers, don't
you know. And then there's the Act of
Settlement ; you can't get over that.'

'I don't want to start any sort of revolution,' replied Mary ; 'though I think you need
one, Duke, to put crooked things straight.'

'Oh, that's all Champion's doing !' murmured the Duke. 'It's he who upsets things.
He has got a bee in his bonnet; he is too clever.
Saxon will find it out. They say he wants to
do away with *us ;* and we couldn't stand that,

don't you know. You should write a book,
Miss Beaton, if you want to put things
straight. The fellows wanted me to write a
book, though perhaps you wouldn't believe
it—about the Turkish war. I was out there,
and I talked to no end of distinguished people.
I could throw no end of light on things, if I
could only remember what they said, but I
can't ; I didn't even put down headings. You
should always put down headings of the conversation when you talk to distinguished
people. The fellows said that if I'd give 'em
the facts they'd work them up, and I wish I
had ; for Bellairs—Bellairs—you know Bellairs
of the Guards ? You must have heard that
he is the most stunning liar—really the most
awful liar. He has written a book all about
the same things and the same people ; and
there isn't a word of it true.'

Mary wished that she had had Bellarmin
next her instead of the Duke of Nornside ;
and Lady Saxon, in arranging her guests'
places, had the amiable intention of provoking
Rolfe's jealousy by the spectacle of Mary
Beaton engrossed with the Duke. So she had
put him at her own table in full view of the

fair Stuart, with the Duchess of Nornside, the wife of a foreign Ambassador, the Archbishop and General Falcon. At the Duke of Athelstane's table sat Lady Struthers, the Ambassador, an ex-Lady-in-waiting, a brilliant American beauty, and a handsome Guardsman.

But Mary Beaton's eyes and her attention had wandered across the table. She was listening to Sir Victor Champion's silvery voice as he assured Lady Eastgrave that French dramatic art is too subtle to be popular in England, and deplored British realism and the terrible system of making points and playing to the gallery. He described Rachel and her exhibition of tragic passion in the famous recitation of Adrienne, a few lines of which he repeated with something of the same magnetic charm as that of which he had been telling. And so on to Bernhardt.

' She is a *maigre*,' put in Lord Saxon, who had joined in the theatrical discussion. ' I incline to the Grand Turk's opinion. I like plenitude and bountifulness in a woman.'

' Oh, she is a *fausse maigre*,' said Lady Eastgrave. ' Her bones are very small.'

The Duke meanwhile had got on to psychology. ' I believe in intuition, don't you know. I buy my pictures and my bric-à-brac by intuition ; and I choose my friends by intuition. I get on ever so much better than the fellows who reason. People who reason always go wrong. There's Champion, don't you know,' and the Duke lowered his voice. ' He reasons. He's a what-do-you-call-it ?— makes black seem white—sophist—rhetorician. *I* never went in for rhetoric—couldn't do it, don't you know. When I'm at the Dilettante Club, and fellows begin about philosophy and Egyptian antiquities and all that sort of thing, I shut up. But I don't make mistakes. Champion does. You should follow out his policy and his mistakes, and you'll find they all come from reason.'

' I don't think he makes mistakes,' Mary said in a tone of grave reproof. ' I don't understand anything about English policy,' she added ; ' but he seems to me to know all about everything.'

' Uncommonly interesting man,' assented the Duke. ' If Bellairs was here, he'd have all that down for his memoirs. It'll be valuable stuff fifty years hence, though it is only about actresses. That's what these literary fellows think of. Why, a lot of headings of conversation of eminent men, don't you know, are as good as a life insurance policy. It might be the Eastern question, you know, and that would be history, paid for accordingly.'

Mary laughed. 'I wish he would say something about political questions,' she said. 'This talk about books and pictures and the drama is charming; but he seems thrown away on such things. He is a maker of history, and I always want to hear him tell of his own deeds.'

'Tell you what,' whispered the Duke; 'if you want him to talk politics, Miss Beaton, I'll try if I can't draw him out.'

'Oh no, please!'

'Yes; you'll see.'

'Then be very careful, or he will see what you would have, and refuse to be drawn out.'

'Oh, I'll manage him all right!' So, by way of managing him all right, the Duke blurted out, 'I say, Sir Victor, what are you going to do with *us* ?'

'Whom do you mean by *us*, Duke?' Sir Victor asked, with a determined smile which had something ominous in it.

'Us? Well, of course, I mean our unfortunate House of Lords. Everyone says you are preparing to make some grand attack on us. Papers all say so, don't you know.'

'I don't read the papers very much,' Champion said.

'Oh, well, they say it every day! They say Tommy Tressel and you are up to something.'

'Fancy,' Lord Saxon interposed, 'Sir Victor Champion and Tommy Tressel being associates!'

'Everyone says they are, though, all the same,' the persevering Duke went on.

'Mr. Tressel,' Champion said gravely, 'is a very capable man, and, so far as I can judge, a very sincere and earnest man. A man may be witty, and may be even cynical in manner, and yet be a sincere politician, Duke.'

'I didn't say a word against Tommy Tressel, Sir Victor. I like Tressel. I like his dinners, and I like his stories; uncommonly spicy stories Tressel tells. And I like

Mrs. Tressel and her stories; she is as good as a play, Mrs. Tressel—uncommonly good-natured, too, don't you know. I think Tressel has some very sound opinions. Had a long talk with him about the Bonapartes the other night, and I quite agree with him that they're no good—ought to be done away with, don't you know. It wasn't I, it was Saxon, who repudiated Tressel.'

'I didn't think he was the sort of man to be in close association with Champion,' Saxon said. He was gazing steadfastly all the time at Champion. Champion said nothing.

'Then you won't divulge your projects in advance, Sir Victor; not even for the benefit of Miss Beaton?'

'Pray don't bring me into so indiscreet a proposal, Duke,' Mary hastened to interpose.

'There is nothing Miss Beaton could ask me that I could refuse to tell her,' Champion said, with a bend of the head and a gracious smile directed at Mary.

'Now then, ask him,' murmured the Duke.

'Thank you ever so much, Sir Victor,' Mary replied; 'but I have nothing to ask, except that you won't think I was foolish enough to ask you anything.'

Champion bowed again in acknowledgment.

'Do you know,' he said, addressing the company generally, 'that I have lately come across a most interesting relic in a rather curious way? It is a bundle of proofs of Walter Scott's " Peveril of the Peak," with Scott's own corrections and additions, and charming little annotations for Ballantyne's instruction ;' and he went on to dilate on the interesting nature of this treasure-trove.

' He won't be drawn,' the Duke whispered.

' Hush, pray !' Mary said. ' You didn't go very well about it, Duke.'

' Extraordinary that such things should get into the papers !' Saxon suddenly said, as if he had not heard a word about the proof-sheets of " Peveril of the Peak." '

' But if they're not true, why don't somebody contradict them ?' the Duke asked, still trying to manage his little game.

'Oh, well, I don't believe in writing to the papers to contradict things,' said Saxon quickly. 'If a man began at that sort of work, he would never get done with it.'

' But there must be something in it all,' the Duke urged.

Lord Saxon looked again at Sir Victor; but Sir Victor either had not heard or would not hear what they were saying. He had now gone off on the question of reputed plagiarism among living authors. Lord Saxon's heavy features wore a look of something like pain. The idea was forcing itself into his mind that his old friend and colleague was keeping something a secret from him for some reason; and that for some reason, too, the secret was partly made known to his wife. But it was quite clear to him that the present moment was not the time for asking any questions, and that in no case could the Duke of Nornside be considered an appropriate questioner. So Lord Saxon tried to appear greatly interested in the subject of reputed plagiarism.

CHAPTER IX.

SIR VICTOR'S MASTER.

SLIGHT lull occurred at Lady Saxon's table while the little passage-at-arms took place between Sir Victor and the Duke of Nornside. Bellarmin noticed that though Lady Saxon smiled sweetly upon the Archbishop, and interjected an occasional remark into his somewhat florid dissertation upon recent archæological discoveries in Central America, her attention was strained, and she was, in reality, listening to the conversation at the other table. Bellarmin, too, followed it with interest, and was for a few moments scarcely so ready in his replies to the frank confidences of his transatlantic neighbour as he

had been at the beginning of dinner. He was particularly struck by the few sentences which Lord Saxon uttered, and by the general manner of his host, which somehow to-night seemed to suggest a greater depth and reality in the man than his demeanour ordinarily indicated. Bellarmin had never known much of Lord Saxon personally. He had always avoided him, having got the idea, perhaps truly enough, that Lord Saxon avoided him. He had made up his mind that Lord Saxon was haughty, self-opinionated, and rude. But quite lately he had found himself beginning to change his opinion. It was clear to him that Lord Saxon liked to be talked to by those who knew how to talk frankly and unaffectedly, and thus to encourage him in talking in the only way he could talk—frankly and unaffectedly. It seemed to Bellarmin that one explanation of that reserve in Lord Saxon, which so many people took to be pride and sullenness, was found in the fact that for Lord Saxon there was no alternative but frank, unaffected talk, or complete and stolid silence. To-night he found himself curiously drawn towards Lord Saxon.

' It would be well,' he found himself thinking, ' for the man who should win and hold Lord Saxon's friendship. And the woman who had won his love ?   If she should lose it ?'

These thoughts were in Bellarmin's mind as the ladies passed out of the dining-room. It was plain that, for some reason or other, Sir Victor Champion had kept Lord Saxon out of his confidence with regard to the move he was about to make.   The question which seemed very doubtful indeed to Bellarmin was whether the disclosure, when it came, would not come too late for Saxon ; whether his loyalty to Champion would stand so much of a strain ; whether he would not feel that he had been deliberately deceived, and would not renounce the political companionship of a leader who had thus slighted him.   Bellarmin thought of his own feelings the other day, and he felt somewhat in sympathy with Lord Saxon—had even a sort of compassion for him.

There was talk of Sir Victor Champion in the drawing-room among the ladies.   Lady Mavis Redhouse reproached her hostess, half banteringly, half in earnest, for placing her in such close proximity to her political arch-enemy. Lady Mavis was a dame of high degree in the Primrose League. She had all the courage of her opinions, and sometimes even flaunted the Primrose skirt. She was poor and proud, and her good looks were waning. She had been for some years a widow, and had apartments in Hampton Court. She had been a great politician, and professed to have carried two counties and three boroughs by her own personal exertions. She detested the Radicals, of whom she believed Sir Victor to be the chief, but tolerated the Whigs; declared a certain admiration for Lord Saxon as being a man of principle, and at heart one of themselves. She was a professional diner-out, and never refused an invitation to this particular house, because, though she inveighed against Lady Saxon's political eclecticism in the matter of her guests, she was as likely to meet a Conservative as a Liberal; and, on the whole, thought it advisable to embrace opportunities for encounter with wavering partisans on both sides, for she liked to be talked of as a wire-puller. People were glad to have her because she was amusing in her way, and she was an aristocratic institution, and would not go to the house of a newly-enriched or ennobled manufacturer or City man : 'No, not if his wife begged me on her bended knees, my dear,' Lady Mavis said complacently.

'I wonder what poor dear De Carmel would have said!' she exclaimed pathetically. She prided herself upon a close friendship with that late renowned Tory chief.

'He would have advised you to make the most of your opportunities,' replied Lady Saxon, laughing. 'Poor Lady Mavis! I must arrange to put you between two Conservatives next time. Only think, Miss Beaton, the last time Lady Mavis lunched here, she had the misfortune to sit beside Mr. Tommy Tressel!'

Mary smiled with grave graciousness, but did not speak. It was not her way to talk much in the company of ladies with whom she was not perfectly congenial.

'Tommy Tressel is a Jacobin,' said Lady Eastgrave. 'I should hate him if he did not tell such amusing naughty stories. But I know that he would put on the red cap in a minute and sentence us cheerfully to the guillotine.   He wants to do away with *us*.'

'Like Sir Victor Champion,' put in Lady Mavis savagely.

'Oh no,' softly interposed the foreign Ambassador's wife, who spoke English with scarcely an accent, and was sweetly neutral in politics.   'Sir Victor has the qualities of a statesman.   Of course, it is his wish to destroy something.   That is the way with them all when they are reformers.   But he is not a Jacobin.   It is only the hereditary right, is it not, that he would do away with?   But,' and she threw up her pretty hands, 'it is a grand power in England—the aristocracy!'

'I am told that in private Champion says he would be quite willing to do away with the Church—our Church.   I have always suspected him of a leaning towards Rome,' said the Duchess of Nornside.   'He thinks it's too troublesome an undertaking, though if he could find a man who would undertake knocking it to pieces quietly, he would let him try.'

'Just as if he were sending for a plumber!' cried Lady Mavis.   'My dear Lady Saxon— don't say anything to me in praise of such a wretch!—he *is* a wretch. We all know it. He must know it himself. He can't help knowing it.'

'Come, now—my husband was a colleague of his—and I am sure you won't say Lord Saxon is a man to patronize wretches,' Lady Saxon said with a smile.

Lady Mavis shook her head. 'Ah, my dear, Lord Saxon will find him out in time. I always said so. He will find him out very soon. There will be a split-up before long. Everyone says the wretch is planning some frightful stroke of policy now—some horrible plot against his own sovereign and his own country. I don't believe he could be happy if he were not doing something to degrade and dishonour his own country. Look abroad! Look anywhere. Nothing is felt but contempt and pity for us—pity for England, my dear, because of that wicked man.'

Lady Saxon, on her part, felt the most utter contempt for Primrose League dames who talked and argued after this fashion. But she had a secret pleasure in drawing the talk out sometimes. And she was anxious, for reasons of her own, to get known as a votary of Sir Victor Champion. 'Perhaps he doesn't mean to be wicked,' she suggested. 'I give him credit for patriotism, Lady Mavis. But what is this great plot people are talking of?' she asked, with a simplicity that seemed delightfully childish. 'I don't believe there is anything of the kind. Lord Saxon would have known; and Lord Saxon would have told me.'

'Lord Saxon! My dear, Lord Saxon is the last person in the world Sir Victor would consult about a plot of that kind. No; it is his policy not to let Lord Saxon know anything about it, until it bursts upon the world and Lord Saxon is no longer able to prevent it.'

'Well, you know everything that is going on.'

'I know most things,' Lady Mavis replied decidedly; 'and so, I think, my dear, do you.'

'All the same, I fancy you are mistaken about this. Tell me—why do people think Sir Victor is meditating any move?'

'Why? Because he appears to be doing nothing. Don't you know that when children are perfectly quiet they are always at some mischief? It is just the same with him. Months and months nothing, or next to nothing, has been heard of him—writing essays on history, they say. Essays on history, indeed! As if that sort of work would satisfy him or his master!'

'Sir Victor's master, dear Lady Mavis—whom do you mean?'

'The devil, my dear—who else?'

Everybody laughed—except, indeed, Miss Beaton; and just then the entrance of the servants with coffee put a stop for the moment to Lady Mavis's anathemas. Lady Saxon moved about among her guests. She talked with much cordiality to Mary Beaton, and asked many questions about the visit to Stonehenge Park, about Sir Victor Champion, about Bellarmin. But Mary was grave and reticent. She could not have defined the feeling which made her shrink from discussing these two men with Lady Saxon, but it was very distinctly present with her. Lady Struthers felt gratified by the demeanour of her young mistress. This stately grace reflected credit upon herself, and was in every

way befitting a Stuart Princess. Certainly
no one would that evening have suspected
the strain of frolic and dare-devilry which was
a part of Mary's nature. In truth, the girl's
mood bordered upon melancholy. She was
a little bewildered, too. Her experience of
English society had so far been limited, but
she found nothing in it that harmonized with
her temperament. The want of reality oppressed her. She seemed to be assisting at
a masque, in which each had a part to play,
and wore a costume appropriate to the part.
She felt a momentary scorn of her own part
and her own costume. What man or woman
with one grain of poetic instinct, with one ray
of ideal craving, has not felt the same when
moving in the world of so-called pleasure ?
The women were narrow and artificial, walled
round by the prejudices of their order, of the
political creed to which they had been born,
knowing no language but the shibboleth that
prevailed in their own particular circle. She
had already discovered that unmeasured re-
probation of Sir Victor Champion was a
characteristic of certain phases of English
society. She had not expected to find it

here, in the house of his colleague and friend. Was sincerity an impossibility with people such as these? Did convictions mean nothing? Was loyalty to a leader only a profession on the floor of the House of Commons?

By-and-by the conversation drifted on to current gossip and scandal—to the talk at Pratts, on a 'society' night as retailed to Lady Eastgrave—so she said—by her husband. She was careful to inform the company generally that he had gone off suddenly on a short yachting excursion. She was sure that everybody must be wondering that he was not with her this evening.

The old Duchess of Nornside murmured maliciously that this view of the subject had not occurred to her; and Lady Mavis Redhouse whispered to Miss Beaton that she supposed Lady Eastgrave wanted them all to believe that the little difference about Count Cania had been squared. The American beauty, who had not long been over, and was in the first modest flush of success, did 'not want to seem too green,' and appealed to Lady Struthers as to what was quite the

'smart' thing to do under given social contingencies, with a frank directness that called
forth the eloquence of that authority on Court
usages.

The gentlemen came in while Lady Eastgrave was giving her views upon a political
conversazione at which she had been assisting, and where a certain Lady Eleanora
Fitzgriffin had made a long Radical speech,
in which she proclaimed that 'the sun of
England's liberty and progress was rising
from the borough of Northampton.

Lady Mavis shook her head. 'Good
gracious ! I don't know what we're coming
to.'

'Oh yes,' Lady Eastgrave continued, 'and
several members of Parliament made wild
speeches, and one man was invited to make
a speech on the strength of his having been
a defeated candidate for a provincial borough.
Why, I have a cousin who actually goes in
for provincial politics, and is standing for the
town council of Manchester !'

'Manchester is rather low form ; but we
must all begin in the provinces, you know,
Lady Eastgrave,' said the handsome Guards-

man, who was thinking of going on the stage.

'It seems to me,' said Lady Mavis, 'that we get everything from the provinces now-a-days. The picture-buyers come from Liverpool, the heiresses from Leeds, and the new peers from Burton-on-Trent. I sat at dinner next to a man from Birmingham last night, and he assured me that nobody ever is born in London now. People all come up from the provinces.'

Sir Victor found an opportunity of coming up to Lady Saxon and saying a few words for her private understanding.

'Everything is going well. I want you to know that; and I shall have Bellarmin with me, I am sure—thanks to you for that.'

'I am working for you.' Lady Saxon reddened under his earnest look, so deeply did the look and the word of recognition touch her. For the moment she forgot her jealousy, her vague distrust. 'You will have more than Mr. Bellarmin with you, I hope,' she added quickly; and glanced towards the part of the room where her husband was standing.

'You hope so—you think so? I am not so certain; but if it should be as you think, then it will be your doing also.'

'No; he believes in me; but he believes in you, too—trusts you, thinks it impossible that you could have any project on foot about which you had not consulted him. He is stupid—ah! stupid enough to kill one with boredom; but he has a sort of loyalty—it's in the blood. It's one of the privileges you Radicals can't despoil them of, Victor. There is something in " race," after all.'

'Could I ever deny it?' he exclaimed, with low-toned warmth. 'The courage of race, the loyalty and chivalrous sense of honour, the *noblesse oblige* traditions—who could deny that such things be?'

He glanced involuntarily in the direction of Mary Beaton. It seemed to Lady Saxon's jealous heart that he unconsciously indicated this girl as the inheritress and the embodiment of true nobility. She lost command over herself for a moment.

'I understand,' she said. 'You have been studying the qualities of race at the very fountain-head. I forgot for the moment that you had but just come from the camp of the Legitimists. Tell me. Are you, too, captivated by the charms of our young Pretendress? She has a long list of admirers, I hear— Bellarmin, Lord Stonehenge, the ex-Prime Minister! In good truth, the young lady has cause to be proud of her list of victims—or should we say her suitors?'

Champion's steady gaze did not falter before the flash of Lady Saxon's eyes as he answered quietly : ‘Miss Beaton could hardly fail to interest even a man so preoccupied as I am. But you, Josephine, know that there is one woman who claims my warmest regard.'

‘Yet you are cold—unemotional,' she whispered passionately. ‘Your letter the other day! It was the letter of a diplomatist, not of a—of a man of heart. Must I still—must I be always a sacrifice to policy?'

‘No—a trusted comrade—a woman who can for the moment put love in the second place. You gave England the first place. Remember our compact. At this crisis you would not have me anything but reserved in my letters to Lord Saxon's wife.'

She changed her tone at once.

'Victor—yes. I will keep to our compact —but—I am a woman!' She gave her shoulders a little impatient shrug and moved towards a picture on an easel, which stood in a more distant part of the room. She appeared to be pointing out its beauties to him, while she spoke in a low rapid tone. 'You must speak to Saxon as soon as possible. If he guessed that Bellarmin had been sounded —that Tressel had your confidence—your hope of him would be at an end. And it is in the atmosphere—you know how whispers are carried by the birds of the air. The papers are full of it. There is a rumour that the Tories want to forestall you. Speak to him at once—vaguely at first. Get his promise. He will be a drag on the wheel, of course ; but trust to time and to me.'

' I suppose you are right—I have no doubt you are right,' said Sir Victor. ' I will speak to him, yes. The opportunity may occur this evening. Better here than in the House of Commons.'

'Yes. I am going to the D'Estivals' ball when these people have left. Will you come on there afterwards, Victor ?'

' I—at the D'Estivals' ball ?   That isn't in
my line, I am afraid.   No.   Let us meet to-
morrow at the House, and take a turn on the
Terrace.'

She gave a little nod of assent.

' It is quite as well that we should be seen
together, especially there,' she said.   ' It will
give a sort of contradiction to these rumours
of a split between you and Saxon.'

She moved away, and began to talk to the
Archbishop.   Sir Victor, too, passed on, and
seated himself beside Mary Beaton.   Lady
Saxon fell into a mood of sullenness, which
was shown clearly enough on her face.   It
was only for a moment, however.   She re-
covered herself and her smiles, and was the
brilliant hostess, the coquettish beauty, once
again.

Bellarmin was by Miss Beaton's side.
The young man's heart had been heavy
within him during the evening; but he
smiled, and jested, and uttered complimentary
nothings, as men and women do in the great
world, even when the fox is gnawing their
vitals.   He had scarcely talked to Mary
that evening until now; and even the little

interchange of commonplaces which had first passed between them had seemed to his guilty conscience a treason to her, and a treason to Lady Saxon. Now they spoke of Stonehenge Park, and of the roses and the lilies, and the walled garden, and the still lake, and of the almost conventual calm which seemed to have settled over everything there, and which had such a soothing effect upon those who came within its influence. Mary spoke with tender regret of the pleasure Monsignor Valmy's conversation had given her, and of the services in Lord Stonehenge's beautiful oratory. It was a trait in the young man's character, that while he professed all the modern materialism, he loved to indulge a certain devotional tendency by dropping in occasionally at the Catholic churches while the mass was going on. The sacred music, the tapers, and flowers, and swaying censers, and fumes of incense, the pageantry of it all, gave him a dreamy sense of satisfaction, and appealed to the mediæval strain in him. He was wont to say that he preferred the music at the Carmelite Church to that at the opera, and that music could only be fully enjoyed in silence, and under accompanying conditions of so-lemnity.

He had thus lightly explained to Mary his presence in the chapel, the first time when she had observed him, quietly seated under the shadow of a pillar, and evidently anxious not to obtrude his attendance. And then she had smiled in grave, sweet rebuke, and had said : 'Ah! the Divine Voice is speaking to you, though you do not know it.'

He thought of her words now, and of the exalted look on her face—a look that he had never seen in the face of any other woman, though he had known several who were good and religious enough, he thought, to be angels on earth.

'Religion is much in your life,' he said abruptly.

'Yes,' she answered with her gentle serious-ness ; 'it is a part of me, or I am a part of it. I mean——' She paused an instant, and then added with some slight hesitation : 'Once, you talked to me of giving up the sham Court and the part of exiled Princess, you called it—and indeed, it often appears to me a sham, and I am weary of the part. That is when the world presses upon me, and I see only the hollowness and the vanity of it; in other moods, I know that there is for me a reality in it which nothing could change altogether. Well, Mr. Bellarmin, I could not tell you, and perhaps you would not understand how the religious feeling is mixed up even with what you call the sham royalty.'

'Miss Beaton,' he said earnestly, 'I used the words only in the superficial sense; I knew that you agreed with me too. It was because I feel so—so deeply about you, and I cannot bear the idea of your being in a false position. But in the real sense, of course, you do come of a line of kings and queens, and nothing could alter what is in your very blood, or make you different or less royal, either by birth or nature. And if you only knew how much I am concerned about you, and how much good it does me to hear you speak in this way——'

'Well,' she said, still hesitatingly, 'you know that it was for religion the Crown was lost; and perhaps it is a wild fancy, but it may be that England will return once more to the faith which made her greatness. Ah, yes, it is so; and she will dwindle and die

new life is not put into her, the life of religion.
I have a deep and a stedfast hope, Mr. Bellarmin. Sometime—sometime—it may be
long hence—truth *will* conquer. It seems to
me that what you need now in England more
than anything is the sense of religion —
such as we Catholics have—some of the old
superstitions, as you would say ; the dear, dead
traditions of your men who lived for piety. I
think England would be greater if there were
more men in her like—well, like Lord Stonehenge.'

'Why do you instance Lord Stonehenge ?'

'Because—I hardly know. Because he is
a very fervent Catholic, and the embodiment
of all that past, all that I am talking of—but
you wouldn't understand.'

'Oh, you must not say that !' exclaimed
Rolfe in low-toned almost passionate insistence. 'I *do* understand——'

He broke off abruptly.

'Madame,' said Falcon grimly at Mary's
elbow, 'Lady Saxon wishes to present the
German Ambassador to you.'

Mary's eyes, which had been fixed on Bellarmin's face in a kind of wonder and tender-

ness, turned away with a sudden startled consciousness. Bellarmin got up. He felt a sick revulsion. Had Falcon overheard his agitated expostulation and guessed the secret his tone might well have betrayed ? It would almost seem so, his face was so thunderous.

Indeed, all the evening Lady Saxon had easily seen that there was something disturbing the mind of General Falcon. The symptoms would perhaps not have been noticed by anyone else ; but they told the story to her. She saw that, for all his effort at politeness of manner, he was unable to keep his attention fixed on the passing conversation, and that he looked anxious and troubled when his eyes rested upon Mary Beaton's face. She saw that he sometimes glanced at herself with the glance of one who has something he wishes to talk about, yet shrinks from saying.

CHAPTER X.

'I HOPE OUR ROADS MAY NEVER PART.'

AFTER a little while the party broke up, only two or three of the men lingering downstairs lighting their cigars and drinking seltzer-water. Champion took Saxon's arm, and in his impulsive, imperious friendly manner led him into a room opening off the hall, which was, in fact, Lord Saxon's study.

'Come here,' he said; 'I want to talk to you.'

Champion flung himself on a couch and pulled forward a chair, in which Saxon seated himself more deliberately. Saxon had one thing on his mind—one only, just then.

'I wonder how these things get into the

papers ?' Saxon said. 'It's rather annoying, don't you think ?'

'What things ?'

'Things about your getting up some scheme or other in alliance with Tressel.' Lord Saxon got the words out slowly, and evidently was under the influence of strong emotion.

'As to schemes, Saxon, a man in my position must keep always looking forward to the future. It is out of the question that things could always remain stagnant as they are. English political life is not a marsh or a dyke.'

'No, of course not. I quite feel all that with you—quite ; and you know that I want to follow wherever you give the lead, if I possibly can.'

'I never could doubt your loyalty and comradeship, my dear Saxon.'

'No; if I'm good for anything, I'm good for that. But it is rather annoying when fellows like Nornside go about telling one of great schemes got up by one's leader and one's party, of which one has never heard a word one's self.'

'You can have the most absolute trust in

me, Saxon. I shall take no decided step in anything without consulting you ; I shall mature no scheme without having your judgment on it.'

' Then you are thinking of something ?'

' Thinking of many things. I have to think of many things. Why, our party has to be literally recalled to life. It is inanimate—all but inanimate. Its lungs must be filled with the breath of a new life. You see that, I am sure.'

' Yes ; I see that,' Saxon answered, in a rather depressed tone ; ' I see all that ; but I want to know what is going to be done before I am asked to do it.'

' Surely you can have no doubt on that point ?'

' Well, that is all I want. I think, Champion, I am entitled to expect that much. I hope I shall see my way to go in any direction just as far as you want to go ; I am sure I shall see my way ; but I am slow, and I want time to think things over. I haven't your inspirations, and I like to talk matters out.'

' A man,' Champion said evasively, ' has to

act sometimes on a sudden impulse, and trust to the confidence of his colleagues, to understand him and his reasons and to go with him, even if, perhaps, they are taken by surprise at the moment.'

'Yes, yes; I admit all that; when a thing has to be done on the moment and won't keep. But that's different, and then all the man's colleagues are in the same boat, and nobody can complain.'

Champion made no reply at the moment; indeed, the Duke of Nornside, coming up with some question, gave him an excuse for not replying. But the impression on Saxon's mind was one of deepening uneasiness. He could not help thinking that something was going on which was kept from his knowledge—not purposely kept, he still hoped and believed. All could be explained satisfactorily in the end, no doubt, when the right time came; but meanwhile he felt perplexed and distressed.

While Champion was talking with the Duke, he made a gesture to Saxon not to move away. Presently the Duke had lighted his cigar and said good-night. He was free again, and able to continue the conversation. Perhaps Champion had not been sorry to have an opportunity of thinking over things. He could think over things very keenly, even in a moment, and even while he was talking with someone whose concerns did not come into his thoughts. Every stranger, man or woman, who got a few moments' talk with Champion, could tell of something delightfully interesting that he said, and tell of the fluency and earnestness with which he had said it. Those who knew Champion pretty well, knew that he generally poured forth this easy conversational eloquence in order to give himself time to think of something entirely different, and in which he felt a genuine interest.

'That man is a bore,' Saxon bluntly observed.

They were quite alone now. All the men had gone. Champion resumed his seat on the couch, and Lord Saxon, after carefully closing the door, came back and threw himself into the arm-chair.

Champion laughed. 'No, no; I didn't find him so. Do you know, I don't believe I ever met a bore. Every man has his uses.'

' I wish I could find that so,' Saxon said.

' Wait till you come to forty years, Saxon.'

' I am not far off forty years,' Saxon answered, not appreciating the reference to Thackeray's ballad. ' By Jove! I mayn't, perhaps, ever get there, all the same.'

' How do you mean ?' Champion asked, in great surprise.

' Well, I have been looking up Scourfield to-day—you know him, of course—and he's been looking me up. And he says I must be awfully careful, and all that; and tells me things are looking rather serious; I must avoid shocks, and a lot of that sort of thing. I have not said a word to my wife, and I don't mean to—just yet, anyhow. It would do no good; the whole thing will probably come all right; even *he* don't say it won't, although he is a tremendous alarmist. So I haven't told her. I tell you, Champion, because if ever I should seem to shirk political work, you will know the reason why, and you won't tell any-one——'

At that moment there was a rustle of silk in the vestibule; the door opened, and Lady Saxon appeared, a radiant sultana carrying a bouquet and a large feather-fan, and with a soft furred wrap falling from her shoulders.

She glanced keenly from her husband to Sir Victor, who had risen at her entrance.

'I see that you are deep in politics,' she said. 'I won't interrupt you. I am going to my ball. Good-night.'

'You are going to your ball,' Lord Saxon repeated mechanically, his eyes fixed upon her. He had risen too. Something in his expression and his manner struck Josephine, and thrilled her with a vague uneasiness. She looked again at Champion. His bland smile reassured her.

'We have been discussing bores,' he said; 'and I have been insisting to Saxon that I do not find even the Duke of Nornside a bore when he talks politics. Allow me,' and he helped her to adjust her cloak.

'Good-night!' she said again. 'No, don't come out with me. Good-night, Saxon— unless I should find you up when I come back. I shall look in here. Meantime, I leave the destinies of Europe in Sir Victor's keeping and yours.'

Lord Saxon went out with her to the carriage. He seemed unusually solicitous about her to-night. When he came back Champion exclaimed impetuously, and with real feeling :

'But, my dear Saxon, what you have told me is alarming. You must have rest. You must not take any trouble or thought about anything !'

'Oh, well, there is no need for being so careful as all that,' Saxon replied with a smile. 'I have no doubt I shall pull through all right, and I don't want my wife to be frightened. She has not a notion that I am in the least out of health.' He was silent for a moment, and then he added, in a burst of frankness much out of keeping with his odd, shy reticence : 'Things would be different with my wife if anything were to happen to me while the Duke was alive, and if I shouldn't leave a son behind me. I've been thinking all day what a pity it was my poor little two-days' old chap didn't live.'

Yes, it was a pity. Champion could well understand that. He had good reason to suspect that owing to the peculiar circumstances of Saxon's marriage, the old Duke had a great deal in his power; and that though under any contingencies Lady Saxon's income was of course secure, her settlements were not so magnificent as would have befitted a future Duchess of Athelstane married in the regular and orthodox way. The childless widow of the heir-presumptive, with no prospect of reigning even as a sort of regent, and no special claim upon the younger brother, who would be head of the house, would certainly find things very different. These thoughts ran through Champion's mind, but he only said :

'My dear fellow, you must not think of such a terrible possibility. As you say, Scourfield is an alarmist—doctors always are ; it is their trade. How many of them have predicted the same sort of thing for me myself! And even he tells you all will be right.'

' Well, that's how it is,' said Saxon slowly ; 'and I think that was one reason why I wanted to know something about what you were going to do. I should like to act with you, and to follow you as long as ever I could.'

Champion paused for a while. He was

really much shocked by what Lord Saxon had told him. He knew that Saxon was neither an alarmist nor a hypochondriac ; and he assumed that Saxon had rather minimized than magnified the seriousness of his condition. He felt a pang of conscience at having kept all his project from Saxon thus far, although he still believed he had good ground for the course he had taken. But he knew that he must say something now. He must tell something—not too much.

'Well, Saxon, I have for a long time, as I think you already know, been turning my attention to the question of reforming the House of Lords, so as to make it a real living institution, and put it in harmony with the spirit of the times. I am convinced that this can be done as a genuine reform, not as a work of destruction. But I also confess to you that I do not as yet quite see my way to the precise scheme of reform which I should like to submit to your consideration. It is of little use talking over mere abstract propositions, especially between men who, like you and me, are, I hope, pretty well agreed as to principles.'

' I hope so ; I hope so,' Saxon said eagerly.

' I am sure of it ; I am for reform, not revolution ; and so, of course, you would naturally be. I am now telling you the direction my thoughts have long been taking ; but I may tell you more ; I have been lately coming to think that this must be the next great reform. Yes, the next ; I acknowledge that I have advanced to that point. But the principles of the scheme of reform—now I wish you would think over them ; think over them carefully, deeply, at your leisure ; and I do hope we shall agree.'

Lord Saxon's mind was greatly relieved. He believed that he was now in full possession of the confidence of his friend. He thought he could easily understand how the mere fact that Champion was thinking over such a scheme had found its way into the perceptions of others, and got crystallized by the breath of rumour into the form of an actual scheme already made.

' I tell you this at once,' he said ; ' I will think the whole thing over, and with a sincere wish, Champion, to be able to help you in your work. I will go with you as far as ever

I can fairly see my way ; and I hope our roads may never part ; I do indeed !’

‘ I think we understand each other, Saxon,’ Sir Victor said ; and then for a second time his conscience smote him. But he reduced it to quiescence and even to acquiescence very soon. ‘Saxon is an overgrown school-boy,’ he said to himself, ‘ with a schoolboy’s pluck, and a good deal of the stolid capacity for dealing with simple subjects which belongs to some of our public schoolboys. He must not be told all until the fighting-time. Murat himself would not expect to be told long in advance when his cavalry were to move, and where.’ This illustration seemed to him effective, and it contented him. But, to do him justice, he was far from content with what he had heard about Saxon’s state of health. There was a curious tradition in the family of the Duke of Athelstane that the eldest son succeeded in two generations, but never in the third ; and the Duke of Athel-stane had succeeded his father and his grand-father. Lord Saxon represented the fateful third generation.

Nothing more was said between Lord

Saxon and Sir Victor Champion that night.
Sir Victor was, on the whole, not dissatisfied
with what had happened.　He would have
preferred to keep all his plans unknown to
Saxon until the moment should come when,
in his opinion, it would be expedient to take
him into full confidence; but as apparently
this could not quite be done, he thought things
had, on the whole, turned out very well,
and that he had played his cards cleverly;
which it always pleased him to think.

Lady Saxon came home comparatively
early from her ball, and she looked into her
husband's study, as she had promised.　She
found him there, alone, sitting in the same
moody and meditative attitude as when she
had interrupted the talk between him and
Champion.

She went up to him and bent over him,
placing herself on the arm of his chair.　The
perfume of the fading flowers she carried, the
rich sensuous atmosphere that surrounded
her, seemed to envelop and partially in-
toxicate him.　He made a little passionate
movement and leaned back against her, his
head resting upon her bosom, without speak-

ing a word. So he remained for some
moments. As she looked down upon the
heavy, flushed face, with its thick red beard,
its drooping eyelids, and rather coarse features, the vision of another face, clear-cut,
refined, pale, and all alight with genius and
sensibility—that eagle look, the silky hair,
the magnetic influence which to her was so
irresistible—a wave of passionate determination swept her being. Yes—every gift, every
allurement of hers should be turned to the
service of this other man whom she loved.
She would crown him, her king of men—and
afterwards—his love. She felt a certain
hatred of her husband at that moment; she
could have thrust him from her with her
beautiful firm arms, which were so strong.
But she wound them round him more closely,
and she put her lips to his forehead. ' Well?'
she asked ; and she could not hide the tremor
of anxiety in her voice—'Sir Victor has gone?'

' He left half an hour ago.'

' And you were talking—you did not talk
about bores all that time? Has he told
you anything fresh in politics? Any new
scheme?'

'Yes; he has told me, in vague terms—there are no definite lines laid down as yet—of his scheme for reforming the House of Lords.   It will be the next great measure.'

Lady Saxon drew a quick, long breath. He felt her bosom heave and her heart beat where his head lay.   It seemed to him that he could hear the heart-throbs loud and tumultuous.

'You are excited,' he said; 'I did not think you took so much interest in the constitution of Great Britain.'

'War-horse scenting the battle,' she answered; 'my wild spirit thrills to the sound of the *fanfare*.   I am ambitious for you, my husband.   *You* cannot be the leader, but he is a great leader; and I want your name to be written with his in history.'

Saxon did not answer except by a heavy sigh.

'And you, Saxon,' she went on; 'he was here to consult you, I suppose—to ask for your co-operation? What did you say?' She caressed him again, and he yielded to the caresses with a kind of stupefying enjoyment, and as though he would willingly have let state-craft go by then. 'Are you in this with him?'

' I have promised that I would go as far as I could. Don't let us talk about it all now, Josephine. After all, it is only in the air, a long way off. Why should you care so much ?'

' I have told you. Oh, it is grand, it is glorious, to see a general making ready for the battle, to see a reformer willing to risk personal popularity, even the break up of a party—for the sake of the reform.'

Saxon seemed to rouse at her words. He moved, releasing himself from her enfolding arms, and turned half round, facing her.

' The break up of the party ?' he said slowly, and with a disquieted look upon his face. ' You must have misunderstood me. The party is agreed upon principles. It never could come to that.'

' It would come to the break up of *a* party, she said quickly, ' if the Progressive Tories joined us.'

'Oh! Bellarmin. Well, I suppose Champion is calculating on that. Don't let us have any more politics now, Josephine ; I am not in the mood, somehow.' He leaned towards her again, and put his head upon her shoulder and kissed her soft neck. ' Tell me that you love me,' he said. ' Seems an odd thing for a husband to want a wife to say, when he is as sure of her as I am of you, I suppose ; but I do want to hear you say it. Tell me that you love me, Josephine.'

' You know it so well,' she answered ; ' but if it pleases you to hear the words, I will say them again and again : I love you—I love you—and again, I love you.'

CHAPTER XI.

TOMMY TRESSEL APPEARS.

THE bells in the churches were all chiming and tolling one Sunday morning after Lady Saxon's dinner-party : the bells in the great cathedrals and parish churches and fashionable chapels-of-ease tolling with deep rich sound, suggestive of good revenues and influential congregations ; those in the smaller Nonconformist meeting-houses clinking in mild persuasive appeal, as if some sense of the old-time disabilities and disqualifications still lingered in their metallic hollows.

This Sunday morning found Bellarmin in his rooms in a meditative mood.   Our poor youth was burning his candle pretty freely at both ends. He had come into public life with a magnificent constitution, which was well-nigh destined to serve him as Gretchen's beauty did her, and prove his ruin. The man who sets out with the consciousness that he has great physical resources behind him is very apt to act on the assumption that they are inexhaustible, and the too-familiar fable of the hare and the tortoise is thus illustrated over and over again in the race between the cautious invalid and the reckless Hercules. Bellarmin loved to tax his splendid powers of action and endurance. He would do everything—would give up nothing. It delighted him to sit up all night at some long exciting debate, and, when the House adjourned, to bring some two or three friends home to his lodgings and talk over things and smoke cigars until the sunlight streamed in, and then to declare that it was too late to go to bed, and accordingly take a bath and start for a walk to Hampstead. He was fond of society ; he liked dinners and receptions and balls. He was fond of dancing as he was fond of riding, and of debating, and of fencing, and of the companionship of pretty and intellectual women. He carried no one liking to excess or extravagance; but the truth is that he was in this one characteristic akin to Goethe's Edward : ' Nichts übertriebenes wollend, aber viel und vielerlei wollend;' he liked far too many things, and he was not always able to contrive to pack them all comfortably and satisfactorily into the compass of his daily life. So he treated that daily life as people once used to treat the old-fashioned carpet-bag : he stuffed in what he pleased, whether the bag was made to hold it or not. He was beginning to suffer tortures about Mary Beaton; and also, it must be owned, tortures about Lady Saxon. There were moods in which he hated Lady Saxon. Again, there were moods of passion and revulsion when that worst half of him, which her influence roused and strengthened, came uppermost and got the better of the purer self. Sometimes he dreamed of Lady Saxon —of his avowing his love to her, and of her returning his words with passionate welcome ; and he cried out in ecstasy, and the dream was gone; and in his first half-waking moment he seemed to see the sweet face of Mary Beaton turned wonderingly, reproachfully on him ; and he called her name and cried to her for pity and forgiveness before he quite knew that he was in his own room and all alone. 'Conscience,' says Scott, 'anticipating time, already rues the unacted crime.' Bellarmin's conscience had no crime on it, acted or unacted, to rue ; but he sometimes suffered as much agony of remorse and shame as if he had actually been Lady Saxon's lover, or had tried in serious earnest to make her love him. 'I don't love her—no—I don't love her,' he would say to himself again and again. Yet when that other mood came, and he was stung and maddened by a sense of unworthiness, he would fly from the thought and presence of Mary as from an accusing angel, and would go and steep himself in the glamour of Lady Saxon's fascinations, would frequent the houses where he might meet her, would follow her at parties and public places. A glance, a smile, a little upward movement of her chin, beckoning to him, would bring him away from any talk in any crowd to get to her side. Lady Saxon paraded him as her victim, and he knew it ; and he was sometimes furious with himself, and yet he had no power to break away. The turn of her neck, the movement of her arms, the rise and fall of her eyelids, sent a fire and a fever through him. All the time he well knew that she appealed only to the sensuous in his nature and the cynical in his mind. But she did appeal to him; other influences, which might have been much stronger, let him pass un-challenged. There were moments when he felt a sort of morbid longing to cut himself off from Mary Beaton for ever, to do something which would make it impossible to have any hope of winning her. Indeed, he had not now any hope of winning her. She liked him; she liked to talk with him—she had often told him so with a friendly frankness which, he thought gloomily, was enough in itself to give death to a lover's hopes. And so there came morbid moments to him when he almost thought it would be well to do something which would put him once for all out of pain—as if anything could put him out of pain—on account of Mary Beaton. Why not marry for money? he sometimes thought, with grim humour. Then he could not rack his brain about Mary any more; and Mary would probably not think enough about him even to be angry with him, or to be sorry for him, or to despise him. Youth finds comfort sometimes in this queer sort of self-torture.

He did not reflect very deeply on the political situation in these days. Lady Saxon was too clever a woman to talk much to him about the Radical schemes, or to try and influence him now more directly than by adroit allusions. She gave him to understand, however, that Lord Saxon had been taken into Champion's confidence, and that the Whig section was prepared to go with the more advanced Liberals. There seemed to be a tacit agreement among them all that he was to be let alone for the present; only there was a grave cordiality and suggestion of friendly understanding in Sir Victor's manner of greeting him when they met in the lobbies of the House which pleased and conciliated the young man more than he would have liked to acknowledge even to himself.

The bells were still ringing, when a rapid hansom rattled up to Bellarmin's door, and brought that young man a letter and a messenger, who had been sent out with an instruction to bear back an answer.

This was the letter which Bellarmin, not without difficulty, contrived to puzzle out:

' DEAR BELLARMIN,

' I want to see you at once ; matter of importance. I have sent copy of this by messenger to each of the half-dozen clubs which I find given as yours in *Dod*. The moment I hear where I can see you, I put myself into a cab and I appear.

' Yours,

' T. T.'

Bellarmin did not need the help—doubtful help in any case—of the cramped and oddly intertwined initials, to know that the letter came from Tommy Tressel. He wrote a rapid line, saying, ' Appear here.' Not more than a quarter of an hour had passed when Tressel appeared. His manner, as an apparition, was in curious contrast with the eager and hurried style of his letter. He lounged into Bellarmin's room with the air of a man who has no thought on his mind but the question

how he is to kill the dull and heavy time.
Bellarmin only gave him a greeting, but did
not ask him any question. Tressel was
finishing a cigarette when he came into the
room. He stopped to light another before
he began.

'Well, it's this,' he said as if he were con-
tinuing an explanation, or answering some
inquiry ; 'Lucifer will be having a fit if he
don't get into negotiations, or communication,
or something, with somebody. So I thought
I'd come, don't you know ?'

This was not precisely clear even to a mind
strung to expectation.

'Come where ?' Bellarmin asked.

'Well, I didn't tell him that ; but I thought
I'd come and see you.'

'All right,' Bellarmin said composedly, and
without showing the slightest sign of curiosity.

'The fix is this : Lucifer is taken with a
sudden burst of public spirit and patriotism,
and that sort of thing, and he still wants to
give the Tories a chance of helping him
in his grand scheme—making it a national
scheme, he says, not the scheme of a party.

All rot, of course; but that's his humour.
Now I happen to know that there are one or
two of the Tory bosses who would like this
well enough if they could educate their party
quietly up to it. I was talking to one of
them, and he wants to see *you.*'

'Why on earth does he want to see me ?'

'Progressive Tories, and all that. He
wants to know how far you would go in the
way of reform, and how many you could
count on bringing with you. He thinks the
House of Lords is doomed unless it can be
reorganized. Of course, I want it doomed
and not reorganized; but I think Champion
has got hold of a good idea for putting new
life into our party, and so I go with him.
Now the question is, Will you see Lord
Twyford? and will you see him to-day—at
once ?'

Bellarmin was surprised, and a little perplexed.

'I meet Lord Twyford in the ordinary
way pretty often,' he said.

'Exactly; but this isn't in the ordinary
way; this is to be in an extraordinary way.
You see, we don't want anything of this to

get into the evening papers. Now if you
were to go and call on Twyford openly,
somebody would see you, somebody would
be there; and the story would go about that
Twyford was trying to nobble the Tory Pro-
gressives. How many of them are you—
five, ain't they?' This was Tressel's familiar
joke about the number of Bellarmin's host.

'But we are on Lord Twyford's side in
politics.'

'Nominally, yes; but you are free-lances
to a certain extent, and nobody knows that
better than the Tories. You may be fighting
for your own hand any day; you may come,
if things run very close, to hold the balance.
These are ticklish times, don't you see?
Everyone feels that Lucifer is up to something; it's in the wind. Now, as he is in this
heroic and public-spirited mood, and wants
to give the Tories a chance of showing how
heroic and public-spirited they are, I suppose
the best thing to do is to let men like
Twyford, who have the brains and the sense,
know what he wants to do and seize the
opportunity if they can. I wouldn't give
them any chance if I were Lucifer; but, then,

I'm not Lucifer, and I'm not public-spirited, and there it is.'

'Still, I can't see why Lord Twyford wants to consult me, or if he does, why he doesn't write to say so.'

'My good young Tory Democrat, it wouldn't do at all. Twyford is very honest and straightforward, they say, and he has a conscience, he says ; but all the same this is a risky business for him, and he wants to look before he leaps. The great trouble is Bosworth. Bosworth hates Champion, and hates reform and new ideas, and so on ; and if he thought Twyford was negotiating in advance with you, the game would be all up. But if Twyford can tell him that you fellows are determined to support Champion unless some terms of reorganization can be agreed on, then, perhaps, he may frighten Bosworth into compliance.'

'Tell me, Tressel, did Lord Twyford say he wanted to see me, and about this ?'

'Of course he did. What else would make me get up so early, and send hunting about all over London to find you ? Six messengers in six hansoms at once !'

'I don't much like that sort of thing,' Bellarmin said.

'Should think you wouldn't. I didn't like it, I can tell you. Put it even at only a shilling each way, that's twelve shillings, and the prices of provisions rising every day,' said Tressel, with a manner of intense simplicity.

'Still,' Bellarmin went on, not heeding Tressel's interruption, 'if Lord Twyford really wishes to see me——'

'Precisely. So I say. That's how I put it. As it is he wishes to see you, not you who wish to see him—I dare say you wouldn't care if you never set eyes upon him again —it's all right then ? You'll go ?'

'I don't know, Tressel ; I really don't know. I feel some difficulty——'

'Naturally -- I always feel some difficulty about everything. But we must act, all the same. Don't you see what a good thing this is for you, who cherish the noble ambition to be a leader of a party, if only of a party of light horse ? Don't you see that it recognises you as a party ? Twyford is a solid man— solid, that's the word—eminently respectable,

going in for conscience and principle, and all
the good old domestic and political virtues;
a man well in the running to be a meritorious
Prime Minister in some quiet day to come—
shouldn't wonder a bit, as things go. Well,
when a man like Twyford recognises your
party as a party, it's a score. Should think
it would please some of your roaring boys,
Bellarmin. How many of them are there?
Five, all told?'

Bellarmin had been thinking of something
of the kind himself, and he paid no attention
to Tressel's stock joke about the number of
what the Paris journals used to call the '*frac-
tion Bellarmin.*' Our young friend had his
weaknesses; and one of them was a certain
boyish vanity about the little party he had
called into existence. The more solemn and
pompous section of the great Tory Party had
hardly condescended to recognise it as a factor
in the political game. Since the days of De
Carmel, Bellarmin had never felt quite certain
whether the leaders of the party understood,
or did not understand, the honest service he
and his band had rendered to what ought to
be, he thought, the common cause. Now

here was, at last, the hand of recognition held out ; in an indirect and furtive sort of way, it is true—but still held out by one of the high Tory leaders. Would it be wise or well to stand too much on scruples, and refuse to see the outstretched hand ? The Earl of Twyford was a man of political and personal integrity ; a man also of honourable ambition ; a little viewy in his politics ; a curious mixture of intellectual courage and moral timidity. He had never been in the House of Commons, his father having died when he was very young, and he had therefore missed all the rough training and practical discipline of the popular chamber. In his earlier career he had bright dreams about the House of Lords winning back its political influence, and becoming once more a real factor in the constitutional problem. He tried to get the Peers to sit longer, and to show themselves active and eager for work, and he started several debates himself, chiefly on Colonial questions, for he had an idea that the House of Lords might assume a sort of moral protectorate over the younger and weaker colonies. But nothing came of it. Irresponsible and elderly

men do not care to take the trouble of debating, when there is to be no result or conse-
quence of the debate. Twyford gave up his
struggle, not without a sigh, and turned his
thoughts in new directions. But it was
always understood that he was one of the
few Peers who would have welcomed some
reasonable and promising scheme for the reorganization of the House of Lords.

'Made up your mind?' Tressel asked.

'Yes, I'll go.'

'That's right. I thought you would.'

'Where?'

'My house. Nobody minds me. It don't
matter who comes to see me—everybody
knows that everybody comes to see me. If
the Pope, the Emperor of Russia and Prince
Bismarck were to be seen on my doorstep arm
in arm, nobody would infer anything. Nobody
takes Tommy Tressel seriously. Shouldn't
wonder if Twyford were to drop in on me at
luncheon-time to-day; he may, perhaps.
Won't you drop in?'

'Yes, I'll come. Tell me—what about
Lord Saxon and the old Whigs? Are they
in this thing?'

'No; there's the fun of it. I have backed up Lucifer in his growing resolve to throw them over. I have told him that it is utterly impossible to think of getting the Whigs over to our side; and that, for my part, I think the time has come when the Radicals ought to decline having anything to do with them. This falls in very well with Champion's humour just at present. He don't quite know what to do with Saxon. Fact is, he despises Saxon intellectually, but is half afraid of him all the same.'

'I rather like Lord Saxon, as far as I know him,' Bellarmin said; 'and now is that dealing fairly with him? Is that quite in accord with the public-spirited and patriotic humour you talk of?'

'I dare say it's partly my doing. I want Lucifer to throw Saxon overboard—show him that we don't care what the Duke of Wellington used to call one twopenny damn—not even a sixpenny or shilling damn, which would be a costly sort of thing, but one poor little twopenny damn—for himself and his Whigs. Then there's nobody else on our side to be talked with. All the rest of

Lucifer's old colleagues are only looking round to see which way the cat jumps. They'll go in for any enterprise which they think will land them on the Treasury Bench.'

'Seems a little like a conspiracy between Champion and some of the Conservatives against Champion's own colleagues,' Bellarmin said.

'Seems like that, does it? No, I couldn't say that. You see, what most of them want is only office, and Lucifer will give them that—if he succeeds—and they couldn't have it without him anyhow. And as to Saxon— Saxon won't take the jump, and what's the good of talking to him?'

'There will be a row when he comes to know of all this.'

'Of course there will; but it won't matter then. It would come anyhow. I have had several letters from Lucifer lately; and the burden of them all is, that never, never, never will he submit to Saxon's dictatorship. I can't find out that Saxon has tried any dictatorship. He don't know or suspect anything about the real meaning of this business. But there is something uneasy about him in Champion's mind of late.　Champion is getting more and more unwilling to have anything to do with him.　I am very glad, for my part; but I am not so sure if it's all right with Champion. I begin to think that I hear a familiar sound —too familiar in politics, my brave leader of free-lances.'

'What sound are you talking of?'

'As if you don't know!　The rustle of the petticoat, of course.　Lady Teazle behind the screen, don't you see?　Champion and she were close friends once—and these old loves renew often.　Don't you remember the story of Millie Moidore when she got married and went off the stage and reformed?　One day her husband thought she had relapsed a little, and accused her.　She owned up handsomely, and said, " You know I hadn't seen him for ever so long, and one must oblige *such* an old friend." '

Bellarmin's cheek flushed.　He was turning angrily on Tressel, and then he wisely bethought himself, and said nothing on that subject.

'Well,' he said, making a desperate effort to conceal his vexation, ' I shouldn't wonder if I did look in upon you at luncheon-time. If any friend of yours happens to be there, of course I shall be delighted to see him.'

'One has to meet all sorts of people,' Tressel replied laconically. 'By the way, how does the Princess get on? Our friend Lucifer seems very much gone there too don't he?'

'I really don't know—I haven't seen—I know nothing about it,' Bellarmin said, with a new flame of anger from a new source. ' Rather absurd, wouldn't that be? Rather a disparity of years?'

'How young you are, Bellarmin!' Tressel said; 'I envy you, by Jove! I, too, can recall to memory a happy and ingenuous time when I really believed it was part of the inexorable decree of Providence that only the young and beautiful should presume to fall in love with the young and beautiful, and that elders—like Lucifer, for example—never thought, except in the paternal sense, of beautiful young women; and that even if they did, it wouldn't matter, because the beautiful young women wouldn't accept their attentions. I am a married man, Bellarmin—

very much married, indeed—and you needn't be alarmed about me. But if I were not—well, I am getting to be an oldster, and you are young; you are a good-looking fellow, and I—well, I'm not a beauty. But I have lots of money, and I presume you haven't a great deal. If you were devoted to a girl—a London girl, at all events—and you asked her to marry you, and I went to the girl's mamma and said I wanted the girl to marry me, how would it end, do you think?'

'I know what you think, at any rate,' said Bellarmin, recovering his good temper. 'You think it would end in the girl's becoming Mrs. Thomas Tressel.'

'You bet your pile on that,' said the genial cynic; and he thereupon took his departure.

Bellarmin was sorry when Tressel had gone, for the terrible struggle between the two natures—between the two imprisoned souls; between the two men, the two creatures in one body—was racking Bellarmin's heart again the moment he was left alone. Again he cursed himself for being in the slightest degree under the thrall of Lady

Saxon; again he felt ashamed of himself; again he almost made up his mind that, merely for being in the smallest way a slave to her influence, he was unworthy to come into the presence of a woman like Mary Beaton. 'To what avail?' he asked himself many a time in bitterness; 'to what avail my hanging on to this girl's train? She does not care about me; she couldn't care about me, even if she could really care about anyone, and the thought of her marrying me is absurd. What should I do with her if she were to marry me? What should I do with a Princess-claimant at my modest breakfast-table; a Stuart heiress to be daughter-in-law to my father; and a claim to the throne of England to be brought on as a Tuesday evening motion in the House of Commons? Anyhow, a man who has sold his soul to Lady Saxon has no business to put himself in the way of a woman like Mary Stuart Beaton. I had better stick to my politics and my speech-making, and my political conspiracies, and mix only with the women who are fit for such work, and are free to make their personal fascinations a factor in politics. That must be my sphere—the only sphere and the only people I have any right to belong to.'

In this genial mood of mind he set out for Tommy Tressel's, to meet Lord Twyford and conspire.

CHAPTER XII.

THE TWYFORD NEGOTIATIONS.

MR. TRESSEL lived in St. James's Square, and when Bellarmin appeared at luncheon-time, he was seated at table with his wife and Lady Cora Mallory, Ross Bingley, the journalist, an *attaché* to the Chinese Legation, and Colonel Towers. Tressel was eating nothing and was drinking only iced water, while the most delicious of dishes and the finest claret and still hock were handed by the velvet-footed servants. But that, as everyone knew, was Tressel's way.

Mrs. Tressel, however, did ample justice to her luncheon; so did Lady Cora Mallory; so, needless to say, did the other guests, except, perhaps, the Chinese *attaché*, who appeared a little bit embarrassed and uncertain how to manipulate his implements, in whose well-being kind-hearted Mrs. Tressel took the deepest interest, openly deploring the absence of edible birds'-nests and sea-slugs, which lingering recollections of her 'Child's Guide' taught her to associate with China.

Mrs. Tressel was a bountiful-looking and bounteous matron, not handsome, but extremely good-natured. She had a certain Malapropian reputation for always getting hold of the wrong end of a story; and a good many amusing anecdotes were told of her, few of which probably had any foundation. There were people who said that Mrs. Tressel's ingenuous good-nature masked all the guile of a woman of the world, and that if she were to disclose all she knew about matters social and political, London society would be considerably disturbed by her revelations. Mrs. Tressel beamed a welcome upon Bellarmin, and made room for him between herself and the Chinaman, from whom she had been inquiring how many wives his countrymen were allowed. She wanted to know all about the

marital arrangements of the Celestial Empire,
and asked a good many naïve questions, when
the Chinese gentleman explained that his
countrymen usually found that more than two
wives gave trouble, and required to be constantly sent back to their relatives as a punish-
ment for insubordinate conduct. Certain great
personages sometimes had four, and the Emperor had six, he added, with a gleam of
national pride lighting a countenance which,
in its immovable gravity, was almost equalled
by that of the host.

Tressel was convulsing Lady Cora over a
witty story with a fine French point which he
drawled out, his eyes half-shut and scarcely a
muscle of his face moving.

Presently Lord Twyford came in ; and he,
too, did justice to the dainty fare, though in
a refined and somewhat abstracted manner.
Colonel Towers greeted the Conservative
chief with effusive geniality, and at once made
a point of jerking political allusions and House
of Commons jokes into the conversation, and
launched into a discussion about the feeling
in the provinces and the Tory manœuvres
during the Whitsun recess, which Lord Twy-

ford laughingly put aside as inappropriate to a Radical table. There was a good deal of light talk, and, of course, Miss Beaton's name came up, and Bellarmin was plied with questions as to the Stonehenge visit, of which all London seemed to have heard. Was it true that Lord Stonehenge was going to marry Miss Beaton? Did Sir Victor Champion mean to play the part of a Bolingbroke and espouse the Stuart claims? What *were* the actual claims?—a forfeited estate sounded *so* romantic, et cetera. And now, had not Lady Saxon taken the Pretendress up, and was she not trying to marry her off to the Duke of Nornside, in order to get her out of Champion's way—for had not all the world read in the society columns of the papers the names of the guests at Lady Saxon's dinner? Had they not even been telegraphed in the English intelligence to America?

Lady Cora Mallory made the first move, and perhaps in *malice prepense* insisted upon carrying off Ross Bingley and Colonel Towers, who she had found out were engaged, like herself, to Madame Spinola for a party on the river that afternoon. Colonel Towers had a shrewd suspicion, notwithstanding the unembarrassed air of Lord Twyford and Bellarmin, that some wire-pulling was going on ; and he would fain have lingered to take such part as was possible in the performance, or at any rate to be in a position to declare his knowledge of the whole matter. Mrs. Tressel discreetly withdrew with the *attaché*, and the other three gentlemen were left alone.

Lord Twyford was a delicately-made and nervous man. He passed for being the intellectual and the educated man of his party ; he had published translations from Pindar and a volume on ' The Science of Thought.' His friends believed that he would be a statesman one day ; he was only just over forty years of age. He had intellectual courage enough to go to the edge of some political crisis ; but then his physical nerves failed him, and he drew back and would not make the spring ; and then he racked his brain for plausible reasons to persuade his friends and himself that he had drawn back deliberately and out of pure statesmanship. At each new venture he said to himself anew, ' I am determined upon it this time; I see my way; I will not draw back.'   Then, when he did draw back after all, he said to himself, 'Of course I was quite right; I only wanted to see if it ought to be done, and I saw that it ought not to be done.'   Still his friends counted on his doing great things—some day; and there was a general impression that the policy which was to revivify the Conservative Party and make it popular while yet Conservative, was to come somehow from Lord Twyford.

Lord Twyford had taken early notice of Bellarmin, and had talked a good deal to the young man whenever he had an opportunity. He admired Bellarmin's talents and especially admired his 'go'—the reckless way in which Bellarmin would fling himself into some Parliamentary gap or at some political obstacle, clearing it by mere rush and dash.   That was exactly what Twyford could never make up his mind to do, and he admired such a quality in Bellarmin as some very weak woman admires physical strength in a man.   Of late they had not met very often, and they had a good many general subjects to talk about.

‘Now if you two,’ Tressel said, ‘would excuse me for a few moments and smoke your cigarettes in happiness, although for the time bereft of me, I should like to get rid of a few letters and messages which won’t well bear delay.’

Tressel’s meaning was quite understood. Lord Twyford and Bellarmin were left together.

‘ Delicious cigarettes !’ said the Peer.

‘ Everything is excellent in Tressel’s house,’ Bellarmin assented.

‘ Yes ; that luncheon now ! Where could you have got anything nicer ?—and the wines ! And Tressel cares nothing for eating or drinking. Gives perfect dinners, and eats none of them. Takes a chop and a cup of tea earlier in his study ! What does our dear Tressel really enjoy ?’

‘ Cigarettes and political excitement.’

‘ Yes, exactly. By the way, speaking of political excitement, ain’t you expecting some of it in your House pretty soon ?’

‘ They tell me so,’ Bellarmin answered. ‘ But we are always expecting something or other in our House.’

'This time isn't there solid reason for the expectation ?'

'Yes ; I suppose so.'

'And don't it concern our House this time ?'

'I am told that it does.'

Bellarmin was perfectly determined that he would not bring the talk to the point. Lord Twyford must do that for himself, or leave it undone. Bellarmin had long been a little uncertain as to the position which he held in the favour and confidence of certain peers high up in the Conservative Government; and he was resolved that Lord Twyford must make the first move. There was a pause, and then Lord Twyford made the move.

'Well, Mr. Bellarmin,' he said, with a little confidential cough, 'I suppose we may come to the point; we understand each other. Champion is planning a great *coup*, and everybody seems to know of it, except—(he! he !)—his own colleague, Lord Saxon. Now the one great question for us is, what are *we* to do ?'

'Exactly,' Bellarmin said ; and he thought to himself, 'So it is *we*, then ?'

'Well, I'll tell you frankly what I think, and then I'll ask you what you think. I quite admit that the House of Lords wants to be reformed—modified in some way. If the change don't take that form, it will take a form less acceptable to some of us. Therefore, I say, let the reform come spontaneously and from within ; let it come from the Conservative party and the House of Lords itself. That is my conviction.'

Lord Twyford's delicate face had quite an heroic look as he spoke. Bellarmin was warmed into confidence in a moment.

'Yes,' he said earnestly ; ' I have long been convinced that the House of Lords must be remodelled, that it must be made capable of development, must be popularized, or it must go. I don't see why it should not freely accept reform, and I certainly can't see why its friends should refuse to listen to a fair proposal.'

' For myself, I should be inclined to go farther. I don't see why its friends should not make the fair proposal.'

' Oh, make it ? Do you think you could bring your people up to that, Lord Twyford ?'

Well, now, there is just the question. If De Carmel were alive, then indeed——'

'Yes; but Mirabeau is dead, as the French waiter said.'

Lord Twyford smiled. 'This conversation,' he said, 'is so very interesting that I think I might venture on another cigarette. Yes, that is, of course, my difficulty; but I am not dismayed by it. We must encounter difficulties—*ne cede malis, sed contra*, you know. They have given up quoting from the classics in your House, I am told. A pity, I think.'

'Come, come!' Bellarmin said; 'we had an Irish Attorney-General there lately who quoted Greek.'

'Did he really? How odd! Well, I see the difficulty, but I don't mean to let it frighten me;' and Lord Twyford looked heroic again.

Still Bellarmin had not got to know exactly what Lord Twyford intended to do, and that was precisely what he wanted to know before he could become quite communicative on his own account. Bellarmin had come, as he understood, to talk over the possibility of inducing the Conservative Government to go into council with Sir Victor Champion as to a scheme for the reorganization of the House of Lords. He had come to think such a project desirable and even possible. But to all appearances Lord Twyford was disposed to go for a project much bolder.

‘Do I quite understand, Lord Twyford? You can only go into this project with Champion or without him. Which do you propose to do? He is in the field; at least, we are assured that he is to be—and he is willing to be our ally—your ally,’ said Bellarmin, hastily but distinctly correcting himself. ‘How do you propose to deal with him?’

‘Well, I’ll be quite frank with you, Mr. Bellarmin. What I want to do is this: I want to screw the courage of our people up to the level of undertaking this reform themselves, and adopting the earliest opportunity of making their resolve publicly known. I want them to announce it in your House and the House of Lords the same night. That would take the wind out of the sails of the Radicals and the Revolutionists! We should gain time ; we should gain everything. We could prepare a scheme at once simple and grand ; I have the idea in my own mind just now—simmering, only simmering—and we should have all the reform in our hands. Well, I have not said a word yet to Bosworth about this. Of course, it's all only an idea yet. It will be terribly hard to screw him up to the proper pitch ; but it will be a great thing if I can show him that the best men of our party will be with him if he will only make up his mind that way. Now I want to know about you and your friends. Will you go with us ?'

' First about Champion. As I understand, you propose to cut him out—that is the plain way of putting it.'

' We are in office, in the seat of authority. If we are willing to accept a scheme of reform, it is our right and our duty as a Government to undertake it.'

' What would Sir Victor Champion say to all that, after his voluntary offer to co-operate with you ?'

' What should he say ? He can still co-operate with us. We, of course, should invite his co-operation. He declares he only wants the House of Lords reformed; he don't care by whom.'

'Yes, men say these things; and, to a certain extent, they mean them. St. George goes out to rescue the lovely—I forget her name—and he asks some hero and brother saint to come along and see fair. The brother saint runs ahead or finds a short cut, and rescues the lovely creature himself. Of course, St. George is very glad that she is rescued; but still, I suppose, he wanted to play the leading part in the drama himself.'

Lord Twyford smiled.

'Your illustration is amusing,' he said, 'but I don't think it quite applies in this case. No man has a right to claim a monopoly in reform. A true reformer ought to rejoice when his work is anticipated.'

'He ought to, and when men are governed by maxims, he will. But that time is not yet.'

'You don't seem very encouraging. May I say that I expected a little more of the venturesome from Mr. Bellarmin?'

'Oh, well now, don't let me be misunderstood. I was only thinking of the matter as between you and Champion, and the difficulty you will have in inducing your people to take the initiative. But so far as my friends and I are concerned, we will go with you heart and soul in any scheme or policy which you are at all likely to sanction. That I can safely promise you.'

Lord Twyford bowed his head in acknowledgment of the promise, but did not seem quite satisfied. He had evidently expected a warmer encouragement. 'You appear to think it will be hard to induce my people to take the initiative?'

'Hard to make them take the initiative!—impossible, I should say; but of course you ought to know all about that much better than I. It seemed to me, that with Champion actually in the field, your people might be induced to co-operate with him—partly to prevent him from doing too much. But as to their being prevailed on to start the thing themselves—well, I can't see it, Lord Twyford.'

'Still,' Lord Twyford said a little peevishly, 'is it worth while taking so much trouble, and risking so much, merely to be Champion's jackal ?'

' A true reformer,' Bellarmin gravely said, ' ought to rejoice when his work is anticipated.'

Lord Twyford's good - humour returned ; and he smiled graciously. ' I am afraid that my people are not true reformers yet in that sense. They will want to be convinced first that the thing is inevitable ; and then, perhaps, if they see that, they will like to get the credit of doing it themselves. But to prevail on Bosworth to accept such a scheme in order that he may become Champion's jackal—well, that would be difficult.'

It was clear that Lord Twyford thought the hour had come for the great deed of his lifetime. Bellarmin could not get out of his mind the idea that there was a sort of treachery to Champion in Twyford's project. That, however, seemed no affair of his. Only a few words more were spoken on the subject ; each man understood the other, and each was a little disappointed. Lord Twyford had expected to find in Bellarmin more of the recklessness of a free-lance ; Bellarmin had expected to find in Lord Twyford less of the craft of a politician.

'Well,' I must be going,' the peer said. 'Charming interchange of ideas ; strictly confidential, of course ; needn't say. Oh, here's Tressel, just in time.'

CHAPTER XIII.

'ANGELS WITHIN IT.'

IT is a pleasant walk through the Green Park into Piccadilly, and thence by Berkeley Square towards Hyde Park. And somehow, about half-past four, Bellarmin found himself in the neighbourhood of South Street, Mayfair; and it was not unnatural, however inconsistent with some of his recent resolves, that he should remember the Benediction service at the Farm Street church, the Catholic church to which Mary Beaton often went. It occurred to his mind that the service would be going on now, and that the sermon would be over by this time, and that the music would have a soothing and satisfying effect upon his nerves and spirit.

So he turned into the church ; and he had not
been seated many minutes before he recognised Lady Struthers' snow-white coiffure and
nodding plumes, and beside the old lady's
portly presence a slender, perfect form, and a
stately little head framed in a coif-like bonnet
and rising above a full dainty ruff, and a
gracious clear-cut face with tender lips, and
deep eyes turned now in calm adoration
towards the high altar, and now bent again in
extremest reverence.

The organ and the choir voices were sending forth a sweet solemn chant, and presently
the pure notes of the soprano soloist thrilled
upward like the song of the lark in its ecstatic
effort to ascend to the heavenly blue. The
candles of the altar were being lighted one by
one ; and they shone in the soft religious light
like stars of a near and mellowed lustre.
There came forth a procession following the
crucifix, before which a gray-haired old man
in gorgeous vestments walked backward, and
after him a file of priests in albs and golden
copes, with tapers, and banners of blue and
gold. The image of the Mother and Child
rising from a bank of beautiful white flowers

was borne aloft while the censers swayed rhythmically, and the incense went up in clouds, and made an atmosphere of heavy perfume. The feeling of unreality which had first oppressed Bellarmin on entering this scene, after the light social talk and the more momentous political conversation at Tressel's house, seemed to fade away and give place to the perception of a consoling spiritual actuality, underlying a certain theatrical effect, which in the Catholic ritual always jarred upon his rationalistic mind. He did not bow his head as the other worshippers did when the procession passed, but he watched it with a vague feeling of wonder and increasing interest, and then an unconsciously deepening sentiment of awe. In his ordinary mood he would have seen a garishness in the gilded images, the starry banners, the gorgeous copes, a sort of prosaic homeliness in the soiled vestments and the crumpled lace of the minor attendants. There was a want of religious enthusiasm in the faces of most of the acolytes; there was something in the whole which, in any other mood than his present, might have provoked him to a feeling of antagonism.

But now, notwithstanding this impression, the ceremonial appeared to him in a dim fashion symbolic of that spiritual essence hidden beneath the outward pageantry and frolic of life —that Divine voice which speaks to the listening soul through sobs and laughter, through the roar of crowds, through all worldly turmoil and clangour. There are moments of brief, sudden illumination, when the eternal truths shine out from the mere emblems, and *It* is there—*It* is with us—the Christ crucified ; the martyred Ideal. For to many the command ' Take up thy cross ' may not be read, ' Crucify the material ; live the higher life in pure aspiration and scorn of the mean and ignoble ;' but rather, ' Crucify for the hour those finer and more exquisite instincts and sensibilities of your nature ; surrender them to the grim, inexorable edict of circumstance, of condition ; of what life and its limitations have made duty for you.'

In condition of mind and soul, of which such mood as this of Bellarmin is but a pale reflection, men of old time walked with God. In these later days of worldly fret, men and women who, in rare moments of exaltation,

recognise the Divine Force working within,
and impelling to faith in the unseen, the
noble, the unselfish, do still hold commune
with God. It would not appear strange to
them, then, were the heavens to open and
the unseen world be revealed; and in very
truth the angels of that world do sometimes
pass in human guise, and, holding forth a
beckoning hand, lovingly bid us draw nearer
to the Holy Presence.

So it seemed to the young man, perturbed
in soul and heart, for the moment irked by the
world, yearning for a higher ideal and for the
purer light which for him shone in the eyes
of a girl. He waited, kneeling, till Mary
came down the aisle. She had lingered in
prayer some moments after Lady Struthers
filed away with the rest of the congregation.
Oh, that one little prayer for him might pass
her lips! She made her reverence to the
altar and walked with eyes gazing straight
before her. She came so close to his bowed
form that her dress brushed his shoulder, and
her little hand, clasping her missal, almost
touched his head. She did not see him.
Her look was rapt and earnest, as if she were

not thinking of the common things of life, with which, he told himself bitterly, he must be associated in her mind. Yet in all its sweetness and earnestness her face was sad, he thought. This angel held out no beckoning hand to him; but he rose at once and followed her closely; and when she took the holy water he dipped his fingers into the font as soon as she had turned from it. He had a glancing fancy that thus some grace or virtue might be imparted to him.

It was not till they both stood outside the church that she turned suddenly and saw him near her. He felt a thrill of wonder and delight at seeing the look of glad surprise which came into her face; it was something more than mere surprise—something deeper and more personal: it seemed a tender and welcoming interest.

She held out her hand, and he took it in his almost silently. Perhaps his face told her something she had not quite known before. Her bright smile faded, and she grew grave in a moment, though not less gentle and tender, and she still looked at him in her clear, questioning way.

'I did not think you would have cared to come to our service in London,' she said.

'I have been lunching at Tressel's,' he answered, 'and I passed by here, and so I went in, and—and I saw you.'

'Mr. Bellarmin,' she said wistfully, 'you look a little worried and troubled. Tell me, is anything wrong with you?'

'Oh yes,' he said recklessly; 'there's a great deal wrong with me. Any sort of life like mine must seem all wrong, I suppose, when one gets under that kind of influence you and I have just come from. It *is* an influence, even for one who doesn't believe in it. But I am not really troubled. I am always happy when I am——'

He checked himself abruptly. He had been near saying, 'When I am with you.' She took up his words simply : ' I, too, am always happy when I am under that influence. Life would be very sad and difficult, I think, without the Church to go to for strength and comfort. You couldn't have come to a better place, Mr. Bellarmin, if you were disturbed or unhappy ; and I think you must have felt it so in your heart, or you would not have come.'

She bade him good-bye, and was moving to her carriage, beside the door of which Lord Stonehenge and Lady Struthers stood. Bellarmin lifted his hat, but did not go near to speak to them. It smote him with a vague pain that Mary had not asked him, as she often did when they accidentally met, to come and see her at some particular time near at hand.

On an impulse he said, ' May I call upon you to-morrow ?'

Mary shook her head.

' I am going to be away part of the time to-morrow ; and when I come home from— from the business I have to do, I shall be tired and stupid, and I think I shall want to be alone ; but come some other day—come soon.'

He took leave of her, and Lord Stonehenge helped her into the carriage, and Rolfe went on to the Park.

The thought of her and of the chanting and the service was with him all the evening, though he dined at a house where he met Lady Saxon. The talk during dinner touched upon the wonder of life in London—its drama, its never-ceasing change and movement, its picturesqueness and its sordid misery, its vivid contrast, its solemnity and its frivolity; the strange beauty to be found even in its winter skies and fog-veiled streets, and leaden livid river; and the subtle fascination there was in its grimness and gloom and mystery for those who had once fallen under the spell of its enchantment.

It was contended that though London possesses a magic as peculiarly her own, and in a certain sense no less potent than that of Rome and other far-famed historic capitals, no poet or romancist or painter has ever completely represented her infinite charm; that poetry, romance and painting have left some of her most peculiar charms untouched.

Someone spoke of the extraordinary variety of feelings which might be evoked merely in the course of one day's experience among the shifting scenes of the great city. Bellarmin smiled a little sadly to himself as he joined in with the speaker.

Later on, he went to a crowded party at the magnificent studio of a noted Academician—a Sunday evening semi-Bohemian party

—where a celebrated French comedian and comedienne played a scene from a Palais Royal farce which had but just escaped the Lord Chamberlain's prohibition, where champagne corks flew, and empty laughter resounded, and beautiful women in art-costumes postured against tapestry backgrounds, and lovers whispered, and art-critics took the opportunity to furtively examine the pictures and appraise the bric-à-brac, and where in dim corners and amid æsthetic groups there hovered that ideal which is exhibited on the walls of the Academy, and sold at Christie's and bargained for by American railway kings, but which had no place in dim churches, and but little affinity with the saints.

Bellarmin flirted and jested and applauded the mummers, with the consciousness all the time of moving and talking in a dream. He looked in towards morning at a late club, and in the gray dawn went to rest and to dream more vividly still of Mary Stuart Beaton.

He had a kind of instinct that the business to which she had alluded was one of her Southwark sister-of-mercy expeditions. He

had heard her speak more than once of the
particular quarter she visited ; and although
he would not for the world that she should
imagine he wished to obtrude himself upon
her, yet somehow, before the meeting of the
House next day, he drifted along the pur-
lieus of Westminster, and thence across the
bridge and down into the Southwark region.
It was a new locality to him, and had a
curious, unaccustomed bourgeois air, very unlike that of the West-End he had quitted, or
the City in all its rush and roar and suggestion of momentous issues and terrific re-
sponsibilities. Bellarmin got into the Borough
Road, where great omnibuses rolled heavily
along the tram-lines, and where carts and
waggons lumbered, but where there were no
private carriages to be seen, and very few
cabs. Then he found himself in a tangle of
lanes and alleys and dismal narrow streets,
pervaded by the smell of decaying fish and
vegetable refuse and mouldering rags—streets
which were mostly given up to the pliers of
petty trades : the cobblers who buy old boots
and turn them out in a wearable condition as
new ; the button-holers, and fish-smokers, and

fur-pickers, and rag-sorters, for whom there is no place in better-class quarters.

It seemed, on the whole, a fairly decent community, in spite of its filth and squalor. The women who hung about the doorways, most of them with babies in their arms, were not vicious or debased looking, but only grimy, and unkempt, and stolid, and miserable, and hopeless. The men looked hopeless too, but few of them were drunken— alas, poor souls ! there was not money enough for the gin-palaces to flourish ! The children were pale and rickety and blotched, as, indeed, was little marvel, seeing that their lives were passed in foul courts where not a breath of pure air might ever penetrate. Here and there, in a more open space, ropes were stretched, and the ragged garments of the population hung out to dry, adding a damp and mouldy odour to the noxious smells that loaded the atmosphere.

Bellarmin wandered on, stopping now and then to give a few pence to some tattered, wistful-eyed girl, or to a group of starved street Arabs, who soon collected at his heels in goodly procession, eager to direct him any-

where that he would go. They were at last forcibly dispersed by a dealer who stood before
his window, in which were displayed a variety
of cheap and common goods—men's shirts of
coarsest cotton at a shilling apiece, and boots
roughly vamped at three-and-sixpence a pair
—and who descried in Bellarmin a possible
philanthropist.

This man was a churchwarden, so he told
Bellarmin, who stopped to talk with him,
and he was, so he said with some pride, the
best-to-do tradesman in the parish ; but he had
his distresses, and just now he hardly knew
how to carry on, for his brother-in-law who
helped him in the shop had run away with
eight shillings out of the till. From him
Bellarmin gained much practical information
as to the ways and wants of the parish. It
was a very poor parish, perhaps the poorest
in all London. The vicar himself had hard
work to live and feed his family, let alone
keeping the church lighted and the things
together, and feeding the poor people.

Things weren't quite so bad as they had
been, though. Once not one of the West-
End charitable ladies, who went down singing

at the East-End, had ever heard of or thought of visiting this God-forsaken spot.   But now —and here a strange thing happened, and Bellarmin's attention was strained to an extraordinary pitch of alertness—now there was a lady, a real West-Ender, and as handsome as a princess; and he didn't know but what she was a princess, for the old gentleman who came with her mostly treated her as such, and old Jacobi, of the second-hand book-stall in London Road, declared she was the walking image of a print he had of Mary Queen of Scots : she had come often of late, and she gave teas to the old people, presents of clothing and prizes to the school-children, and it was all through her that the soup-kitchen and the *crèche* had been started. The man went on to tell him that she was there that very day; that she was at the school-house now with the vicar and some other gentlemen, one of whom—and the dealer looked mysterious—was uncommonly like the pictures in the *Comic Illustrated* of Sir Victor Champion.   The dealer didn't know as he had any politics himself; he had voted for the Conservatives last election, because they'd told him as he ought to stand by the country ; but if the Liberals was going to do better by that parish, why he was willing to let Sir Victor have his vote, and it wasn't much odds any way ; and if Bellarmin would like to see for himself that the people were not such a bad lot, taking them all round, he had only to look into Green's Gardens, where he would see an average selection.

Just then a customer came, and Bellarmin, who really wanted to know what manner of people these were to whom his Lily Queen devoted herself, asked one of the urchins to show him the way to Green's Gardens—a row of dingy, miserable, dilapidated two-storied houses, looking out upon a foul, ill-smelling court, and offering melancholy satire upon the bare suggestion of flower-beds.

There was a little flutter of excitement about the place, however, amid all its wretchedness. Bellarmin was not long in discovering the cause. Had not his Princess passed that way ? In good truth it might well have seemed to the dwellers in that dreary street that angels were abroad upon this soft June afternoon. It was not difficult to identify the 'beautiful lady' who had come to the rescue last week, when the gaunt, hard-worked mother of seven, in No. 5, broke her mangle, her only means of earning a scant subsistence, and whom starvation threatened, till by some miracle the mangle could be repaired. The angel had performed the miracle, and the mangle was at work again. And then there was the decrepit cobbler, who had started in life afresh now that 'the lady' had provided him with tools and leather. And there was the deaf widow, who used to support herself handsomely by making band-boxes, till, as she grew deafer, the shop people lost patience and refused her orders, until 'the lady' came and went herself to a great warehouse, and somehow managed to get the poor old dame a certain weekly order for the few dozen that she was able to turn out.

And then there was the family which were to be emigrated to Australia, whose passage she had paid, and whose clothes she had taken out of pawn; the head of that family never quite knew how it was that he became the possessor of a little nest-egg which the vicar handed him before he sailed, as the gift

of an anonymous friend. It must be owned
that Bellarmin's impulsive liberality that day
was somewhat in ratio with the blessings
poured upon the beautiful lady whose name
and position no one seemed to have exactly
ascertained. But, anyhow, some hopeless
hearts were gladder, and some starved bodies
more content that night, because of what he
had done.

When he had visited most of the dwellers
in the Gardens, he made his way as quickly
as he could towards the Borough Road again.
He had a nervous dread lest Mary should
see him, or get to know of his presence there.
By chance, however, he struck upon a little
square with a church and a red-brick school-
house, and more lines and more clothes
fluttering in the wind; and as he passed at
the end of the square the faint sound of a
sweet, fresh voice that he knew fell upon his
ear, with just that little imperious intonation
in it which told that his Princess was at
that moment very earnest and intent on the
carrying out of some project for the people's
good.

Bellarmin could not but pause and look

from behind his screen of bulging sheets. She was there, standing very straight, and looking very slender and stately, in her plain black dress and little close bonnet, and with a part of her profile only visible to him. There was quite a group of them, just outside the church door. General Falcon stood by, and Sir Victor Champion; yes, there could be no doubt about that. His face was turned towards Mary, and had a look of deep attention, as if he were revolving her project, whatever it might be, in his mind, and taking all its practical bearings, before he flashed into enthusiastic advocacy. Bellarmin had often seen the same kind of look on his face in the House of Commons, only that then it had not the tinge of strong personal interest which warmed it now. Bellarmin felt a darting pang of jealousy. If *he* were on the eve of becoming Prime Minister, and had a great fortune, and might not only restore to the last of the Stuarts her forfeited inheritance, but take from her counsel and inspiration, and perhaps bring into practical working some of her visionary plans for the good of England—— Ah, well! he was glad for

Mary's sake that she had enlisted interest so powerful.

There was no doubt that if Champion, as Prime Minister, were to urge Mary's claims in the House, they would be carried. Liberals and Tories alike would be fired to an impulse of generosity towards one so beautiful, winning, and so good. The act of forfeiture would be reversed in a manner becoming in a magnanimous Government, and a wise and lofty-minded sovereign absolutely secure of the affections of her people, and able to smile at the bogie of a Stuart pretender to the throne. Then all this shadow and sham and net of intrigue and assumption would fall away from Mary. Her claims having been recognised and acceded to, she would stand forth in an assured position, free to live her own life and do her good works as she pleased. Ah, yes! he was glad—very glad. But he wished that he could be the great Minister, and that it might be in his power to do all this for her.

A clergyman in a long rusty coat and felt wide-awake—evidently the vicar of the parish —was in the group : a man with a tired, com-

monplace face and stooping gait, and eyes
alight now in wonder and hope, as he glanced
eagerly from Miss Beaton to Champion.
Probably he, like the dealer, would be quite
willing to turn from Tory to Liberal, if the
latter party were likely to do better than the
former by that particular parish.   Then there
was a little woman in brown alpaca and a
shabby bonnet, twinkling with jet—a school-
teacher or district visitor, probably—all agape
with astonishment and delighted expectation,
who would put in her modest word when Sir
Victor asked the vicar a question, and he
turned to her.   They were all in full conclave.
Bellarmin wished that he could hear what it
was about, and wished, too, that he might
join in it.   It was only a very little reform, easy
enough to a rich philanthropist, and scarcely
involving a question of legislation, though
Mary, in her anxiety, felt sure that an Act of
Parliament might be passed immediately to
set everything right.   It was only about the
starting of free breakfasts for the hungry
scholars whom a beneficent State provided
with a mass of valuable knowledge, but
whose empty stomachs were not equal to the

task of assisting their minds in its digestion. Had Bellarmin gone boldly forward he would have been welcomed, and he might have secured for himself several opportunities which fell to Champion of enjoying Mary Beaton's society, and benefiting his fellow-creatures at the same time. But he felt sore and sad, and he turned quietly away behind the sheets, and wandered out of the labyrinth of alleys by a different path.

END OF VOL. II.

BILLING AND SONS, PRINTERS, GUILDFORD.

9 783337 051365